"Something About Us"
A Lesbian Romance

Jenny Bloom

© 2019
Jenny Bloom

All rights reserved. No part of this publication may be reproduced, distributed, or transmitted in any form or by any means, including photocopying, recording, or other electronic or mechanical methods, without the prior written permission of the publisher, except in the case of brief quotations embodied in critical reviews and certain other non-commercial uses permitted by copyright law.

This book is intended for Adults (ages 18+) only. The contents may be offensive to some readers. It may contain graphic language, explicit sexual content, and adult situations. May contain scenes of unprotected sex. Please do not read this book if you are offended by content as mentioned above or if you are under the age of 18. Please educate yourself on safe sex practices before making potentially life-changing decisions about sex in real life.

This story is a work of fiction. Names, characters, businesses, places, events and incidents are the products of the author's imagination or used in a fictitious manner & are not to be construed as real. Any resemblance to actual persons, living or dead, or actual events is purely coincidental. Products or brand names mentioned are trademarks of their respective holders or companies. The cover uses licensed images & are shown for illustrative purposes only. Any person(s) that may be depicted on the cover are simply models.

Edition v1.00 (2019.01.28)
www.JennyBloomAuthor.com

Special thanks to the volunteer readers who helped with proofreading. Thank you so much for your support.

Chapter One

It was the first time in a month that Bailey had a chance to go to the bar. But, since she was bulking now, she didn't have to worry about how many carbs she could have. Instead, she increased her calories and lifted heavier, and she was quite happy with the changes she saw.

Plus, it was the first Friday night in weeks she didn't have clients. They would start to peter out over the next couple of weeks, mostly because the holidays were approaching, and most had families to attend to, so she would get most evenings off. Which was nice, because Bailey needed a break. Being one of the best personal trainers in the city was hard, but she was dedicated, and her clients loved it.

As she drank her vodka with seltzer, she looked around. The bartender smiled at her when she set the drink down.

"Got any cool plans for the holidays, Bailey?" he asked.

"Nope. You, Neal?" she asked.

Neal was one of her clients, and a bartender she grew to be friends with. He liked working on lifting, and the two of them got along great. Plus, he knew that she wasn't interested in dudes, so unlike some idiots she worked with, Neal understood his boundaries, and as he looked at her, he nodded.

"Yeah. I have a date with some girl a couple days before, and I get to see family. You?"

"Nothing this year. As usual. My family is still mad that I chose to be a personal trainer instead of working at their investment firm. But I'm shit with numbers, and the last thing I want to do is sit on my ass all day doing something I hate," Bailey replied.

"I feel that. I mean, that's why I'm here and not working in my dad's shop. Sometimes you gotta do what you gotta do. Anyways, if you want to, you're always welcome to come to my place for the holidays. I'm sure that my parents will understand," he said.

"It's fine. I'll probably just use that day like I always do. I'll just go to the gym and lift," she said.

"Well I mean, if that's good for you, then that's good for you. But, if you want to have a good Christmas, you're always welcome," he offered.

"The last time I had a normal Christmas was so long ago, I wouldn't know what to do. There're a few weeks anyways. I mean, I'd be lucky if a fucking miracle came along and plopped itself right in front of me. Working out has always been super easy for me, but dating, not so much," she explained.

"I get that. Can relate. But, good luck out there," he said.

"Thanks. I'll need it."

It wasn't like Bailey had a terrible life. She just didn't feel a connection to others, period; especially when it came to love. Hell, the last time she felt it, she almost confessed to the girl who meant the world to her, but she stopped herself. It would've been too much, and she was pretty sure that she was gay anyway.

It's not like she would plop herself down, right in front of Bailey, right?

As time passed, Bailey sighed. She didn't think anything would happen. She had such a successful business, it was something she felt blessed with. But, at the same time, things felt...empty. She felt like she was missing something, whatever it might be, and that's what bothered her the most about this.

Suddenly, she felt something strange. It was like a change in the atmosphere, and when she looked up, she saw the most beautiful blonde she ever laid eyes on. She felt her heart race, skipping a beat, and suddenly, she felt completely immobilized by this woman's demeanor. She couldn't believe how pretty she was. It was almost as if it was a crime to be so beautiful.

But, as she drew closer, there was a familiarity to her. When she looked at Bailey, she grinned immediately. Bailey thought the world had just changed, and that fate was playing some cruel joke on her.

"Hey Bailey, very-long-time no-see," the voice said.

She moved to Bailey, who had a look of shock on her face. She tried to make it go away, but it was no use. She couldn't stop looking at the beautiful woman, transfixed by her beautiful eyes and the way her body looked. She had the same beautiful eyes that Bailey loved to stare at back in the day. And, although it had been five years, Bailey realized this woman didn't look much different than when they parted ways after graduation.

"Melanie..." she finally said.

"So, you do remember. I thought I would need to jar your brain. You look like you've seen a ghost or something," she teased.

"I mean, I wouldn't say you're a ghost, but you're someone I honestly forgot about; someone I thought I'd never see again," Bailey admitted.

"Gee, nice to see you too," she teased.

"Sorry, it's just...so shocking honestly. I'm really glad though," she admitted.

Bailey didn't know how to put the words together, but then, after a moment, Melanie spoke.

"By the way, are you here alone? I just came here because I needed a break from my family. If you want, we can chat, just like old times," she offered.

Like old times. Bailey never thought she would get a chance like that again. The sounds of the bar were inconsequential compared to Melanie's beautiful voice.

"I mean sure, I'd love to catch up. I didn't think you'd ever come back here," Bailey admitted. She looked at Melanie, who was smiling with a beaming grin.

"You'd be surprised by how long I'll be here then," Melanie replied.

Bailey looked at her with confusion, unsure of what she meant by that.

"Wait, you don't mean--"

"Yeah. I'll be here for at least a month. I needed a break from modeling. I've been feeling a little all over the place, and I just...I need a break," Melanie said.

"What kind of break?"

"Just a break from the world of modeling. I've had some personal issues that I've been worried about lately, and it's been driving me crazy. I've also had a lot of feelings eating away at me, and I feel a little lost," Melanie explained.

Bailey could relate.

"I feel you. I've been in a strange place myself. But, you'll be here for a bit, right? Do you have plans for Christmas?" she asked.

"I don't. I was just planning to see family. What about you?"

Bailey shouldn't have been surprised that Melanie had no idea about her family situation, but she simply shook her head.

"I've celebrated the holidays alone the last few years, since I decided to pursue a career in personal training. My family wasn't too happy about that, among other things, so I've been on my own. Needless to say, I miss having that support network. But, they didn't accept me for who I was, so I told them I can't be their kid if they don't accept me for me," Bailey said.

There was a lot more to it, but Melanie seemed to relate.

"I understand. I mean, my family has been supportive, but it's a problem for me too. I want to live my own life, but I know what they will do if I tell them things; they'll just drop me. I don't really like the way they view my life, but it's not like I'd really be doing much else," Melanie said.

"Are they not happy with the modeling?"

"Yeah, but they typically just push me into gigs and shit. I don't really want to do it anymore. The world is too stressful, with obsessions about what I need to eat, what should have to wear, and where I need to be. I don't really know what else I can do about it, other than just keep doing it," Melanie said.

For Bailey, she understood the annoyance that her friend felt. After all, it was obvious Melanie was happy for the first time in a while.

"Well, if you want to get away from your shitty family, you can always come hang with me. I wouldn't mind going out and shit too. I've been working, but I've got a small lapse between clients. I feel like it may be best that we do this together. If you want to hang out, that is," Bailey said.

She looked at Melanie, unsure of whether the other girl would take her offer or not. But Melanie was definitely smiling, and Bailey felt better about it.

"Yeah. By the way, are you gonna stick around for a bit?" she asked.

"Yeah. You?" Bailey replied.

"I want to. It's nice being around someone who isn't telling me where I need to go, and pushing me into some bullshit that, ultimately, won't make me happy. It's just...nice, that's all," Melanie said.

Bailey could tell from the serene expression, even with her eyes closed, that Melanie was much happier here than doing any sort of modeling bullshit. It made her feel happy, and she wondered what might make Melanie happy next. Bailey felt good. No matter what happened next, this could be the beginning of something. Though, what that would be, she wasn't so sure of.

Chapter Two

Melanie felt happier than she had in a long time, simply from sitting and talking with Bailey. Although it was surface conversation, there was a sense of happiness she didn't normally feel. She could see from the widened eyes and happy expression Bailey had, that Bailey was happy to be with Melanie also.

It was the first time she'd seen Bailey since graduation. After graduation, they hadn't said a word to one another. She always wondered why Bailey grew distant after they left high school. Melanie figured it was because of their different pursuits. Melanie went straight into the world of modeling, and some schooling on the side, which sat on the back burner. Meanwhile, it seemed Bailey had her whole life together, and it made Melanie happy, albeit a tad bit jealous.

"I'm surprised you've got your shit so together," she said.

"It's not really the case for me. I mean, I just work a job where I have a lot of clients. It's simple, but it's also good for me. I mean, I love training my body, and lifting a lot, and I feel that helping others with do it is ultimately what I want to do."

"Good. I'm glad. I mean, I wish I had that much drive with modeling. It pays well, and I do love it, but it's also stressful," Melanie admitted.

That wasn't even the half of it. There was a reason she kept her phone off.

"Maybe I can help with that stress. Do you go to the gym at all?" she asked Melanie.

Melanie shook her head.

"No. They want me to have a certain look, and they don't really want me going to the gym and getting toned."

"That's bullshit. You don't magically get big and bulky, Mel. The reason I am is because I've been training and working with heavy weights for a bit," Bailey said.

"Yeah, I figured. I just feel stressed. I'm always under the eye of my parents; this is the first time in a while I've gone out to a bar. They don't know, they just assume I went to town to look at the Christmas lights, but I needed a fucking break. It's too much for me," Melanie said.

She looked at Bailey, and suddenly, the muscular woman extended her hand to touch Melanie's thigh.

"It's okay. Trust me on this. You're safe with me," she insisted.

Melanie felt a twinge of happiness when she heard those words. Bailey was so sweet to her, and it shocked her to the core that she would be so nice.

"You're still the nice woman you always were, Bailey. Always supportive of me," Melanie said.

"I always will be Mel. Trust me, you mattered a lot to me, and I'm sorry I fell out of touch," Bailey said.

"There had to be a reason why, or so I figured. I had my own reasons as well. Besides work being stressful as hell," she said.

When she looked at Bailey, she felt her heart skip a beat. She craved the feeling of closeness once again, and wondered if they could go back to being the friends they were before. Melanie honestly didn't know. They had gotten older. It had been five years. Melanie knew being a model wouldn't last forever, and she could tell that Bailey was happy, but there was something missing in her life.

"If you want, we can hang out. There's this little Christmas market we can go to. You know, as friends. And I wouldn't mind going ice skating with you either. It can be like old times. That is, if you want that,' Bailey said.

Melanie wanted it. She wanted to stay out of her parent's home, away from the stress, and away from the clamoring from both individuals who always wanted her working. She yearned for this, and with a smile on her face, she nodded.

"Yeah, I'd love that. You know, I haven't had a conversation like this in forever Bailey. It's refreshing, in all honesty," Melanie said.

Melanie knew for a fact that Bailey was happy to be near her, but she felt that there was a wall there. Maybe it was Melanie's imagination, but she felt a strange desire to be near Bailey, but also a fear of what it might mean.

The truth was, Bailey meant a lot to her. She thought about her a lot. There were quite a few times she had found herself holding the phone in her hands, thinking about dialing Bailey. But, she never did. This was a chance encounter, and she was so happy that Bailey agreed to this. It made Melanie's heart happy.

"Same here. I'm just surprised you want to talk to me, that's all,' Bailey admitted.

"You're like my best friend from high school Bailey. I'm more upset we didn't talk afterward," Melanie said.

"It was my fault. I had my own hesitations," she admitted.

Melanie could tell there was something eating away at her, but she didn't want to pry.

"Well, whatever it might be, I'm happy that you're here now, and with me," Melanie said.

"I am too. Thanks," Bailey replied.

"No problem. What are friends for?"

The rest of the night was spent talking and laughing like old times. It was dumb conversation, but Melanie craved this. It was the first time in what seemed like forever that she finally got to express herself. She knew how stressful this might be for Bailey too, but it was weird, they picked up where they left off like it was nothing, and Melanie adored that. It was different, for sure. She couldn't lie, she did feel her heart thump in her chest as they talked, and she wondered why that was.

She always gravitated toward Bailey. There was something so cool about her. It made Melanie smile.

"You know, you've only gotten stronger since high school. I remember you were like the top player on the basketball team," Melanie said.

"Yeah, and you would come to my games to cheer me on. Miss those days, but basketball after high school is rough. So, I did the next best thing,' Bailey explained.

"Seems like you do it well. You look amazing," Melanie said.

It was then when the awkward silence hit. She never complimented Bailey like this before. But when Melanie looked at her body, eying her taut muscles that were strong, but also feminine, and her body that was curvy and something she dreamed of, Melanie felt a thought ghost past her mind.

Bailey looks really hot.

Melanie blushed, and suddenly, she noticed Bailey's eyes on her.

"What are you blushing for?" Bailey asked, her voice quiet and slightly nervous.

"Sorry, I was just admiring how, well... beautiful you've become. I'm sorry, that probably sounds fucking weird," Melanie said.

"No, it's fine. You're the beautiful one Melanie. I would kill to have your looks," Bailey said.

"But you're so muscular and beautiful. It's nice to see," Melanie said.

"Aww. That's sweet,' Bailey replied.

The awkward air dissipated with that, and they continued to talk like old times. But Melanie wondered where that thought came from. She never regarded her best friend like that before.

It's not like Melanie wasn't attracted to women. She found the female form pretty, and never really had the desire to pursue a boyfriend. But the fact that her eyes kept gazing over Bailey's body, staring at her curves, made Melanie's heart race, and there was an obvious desire there.

Fuck, she needed to get her mind away from this before it went completely into the gutter. About three hours had passed since she got here, and it literally felt like no time at all. She missed this type of conversation, especially with her best friend.

"Shit, it's late. I should be going. My family will be wondering where I am," she said.

"Understandable. Say, do you want to go ice skating tomorrow? It could be fun," Bailey offered.

Melanie blushed, but then, she nodded.

"Yeah, I'd love that," she admitted.

"Good. It's a date then."

With the utterance of those words, Melanie grew red. Bailey said the word date, which normally wouldn't make her body heat up and her face flush, but there was something about the way she uttered it that made Melanie immediately tense, and suddenly, she smiled.

"You're right. It's totally a date. See you then," she said.

The look on Bailey's face at her affirmation made Melanie want to giggle like a little girl. This woman was her best friend, and Melanie wanted nothing more than to spend time with Bailey. It wasn't like she had a crush on her or anything, she just felt happy and secure that Bailey was back, and the two of them could have a normal relationship.

Right? It wasn't anything more than that, and she was happy with it.

But, as Melanie went to her car, she felt the excitement growing in her body, heating up at the thought of spending time with Bailey.

Chapter Three

Bailey prepared to leave the bar, but before she left, she heard Neal whistling from the other side.

"Cut it. I know that I was flirting with her," Bailey said.

"If you didn't realize it, she was flirting with you," he told her.

Bailey blushed. "No way. She's not like that. She was probably just happy that she had someone to talk to. Sounds like the modeling world is fucked right now," she replied.

"No, if you didn't realize it, she got red as a tomato when you said it was a date. Kind of cute, if I do say so myself," he said to her with a smirk.

Bailey didn't believe it. In truth, she loved the fact that Melanie stuck around to talk. She thought that Melanie would have left after a few minutes, but their conversation went on forever. Bailey sighed, unsure of how to feel.

"It's like old times but...I'm worried about what this might mean for us," she explained.

"Bailey, do you realize you have a girl in front of you who is a total cutie who wants you, but is afraid to admit it? I could tell she was embarrassed, and she was totally checking you out. I don't have to be an expert on gay relationships to know that she has the hots for you. You should go for it," he said to her.

Bailey thought about it. She wouldn't mind at least having a little fling. But, would Melanie really want something more? That's what worried Bailey the most.

"I wouldn't mind having something more with her, it's just...I worry what might happen between us. I mean, she's got her own goals, and I have mine. I don't know if we would work well together or not," she admitted.

"You never know unless you try," he offered.

She nodded, feeling slightly worried about where to go from here.

"I'm worried because I never told her my feelings. Truth is, I've liked her for a long time, and I almost confessed the night before graduation. But, I felt if I did, I wouldn't really be able to have that type of relationship with her. I know she's extremely pretty. She's super popular. Which is why I kept my distance. I always knew she would go into modeling as well, so I knew my place," Bailey said.

"You're both older though, and it's pretty obvious she doesn't want to model for much longer. Sounds like she needs you," he said.

"Yeah. I feel like she might. I'll see how this goes. We went ice skating together years ago, and she would always cling to me, so it was a sweet gesture. I wonder sometimes, what would've happened if I had kissed her that day, though; if I told her everything," Bailey admitted.

There were many worries she had; different considerations that she felt about them being together. But then, Neal scoffed.

"You gotta go for it. Come on, you're always pushing me, so it's high time I push you back," he told her.

She smiled. "Thanks. Maybe, one day, I'll be able to face my parents again and tell them how happy I am. Maybe then I could live a more fulfilled life," Bailey said.

She hadn't talked with them in years, not just because of coming out; it was so much more. She felt better though, after talking with Neal, feeling some renewed happiness as well.

"You deserve to be happy, girl. I can tell you've got a lot on your mind, and a lot that you need to do, so just go for it," he said.

"I should. Thanks," she replied.

"No problem. You can do it," he said.

She nodded. She knew that she could do it, but it was a matter of how she could. After she left, Bailey went back to her apartment, noticing as she arrived that Melanie had sent her a text. She read it, feeling the butterflies in her stomach grow once again, the desire to say more on the tip of her tongue.

Hey girl. I had a blast tonight, and really can't wait to see you tomorrow. This is the type of break I need.

Bailey smiled to herself, feeling better about everything that transpired. She knew this was the right thing to do, even though she feared what might come next. She texted Melanie that she had a blast as well and couldn't wait to see her tomorrow either. As she closed her phone, she sighed.

Things were getting better. She knew this, but there were so many different thoughts in her mind about it, that it made Bailey nervous. Would they really work this out? Could they? In truth, Bailey didn't know. She feared what the future might bring, but if this turned into a Christmas gift for herself, she wouldn't complain.

Chapter Four

When Melanie got back, she could still feel her heart racing. She wanted to spend more time with Bailey. It was strange, like there was some sort of force grabbing her and holding her there.

When she got inside, immediately her mother walked up to her, sighing.

"You were out late," she said.

"I was out by myself. Met someone. It was nice," Melanie said.

"Well, don't let some guy get in the way of your goal. You're a model first and foremost Melanie, and you can't spend time with just anyone," she chided.

"I'm not. I wanted to see someone, and I did. Lay off," Melanie said.

"I will when you get out of my home and get back to modeling. This break better be a temporary thing," she said.

Melanie hated that her mother was so insistent upon her being a model. Sure, she was supportive of her during her formative years, but now, she was almost obsessed with it, . and it made Melanie want to do nothing more than quit.

"It's Christmas-time. I need a break," Melanie muttered.

"You say this, but it's obvious that you're just delaying the inevitable," she said.

"I just need some time alone. Jesus," Melanie said.

She was so sick of her mother always pushing her toward like this goal. She hated how overbearing she was, and at the back of her mind, she felt a little bit jealous of Bailey. She stood up to her parents, and she made it look easy, so she didn't really have anyone bothering her.

Melanie wanted more than anything to get out of the modeling business. It was cutthroat, and she felt the stress grow increasingly.

"You didn't eat too much, did you?"

"No Mom. I just went out and had a bit of fun. Lay off me. I'm going ice skating tomorrow too," she said.

"Good. You should get exercise. But, don't get big. People don't want to hire manly-looking female models," she said.

Melanie looked at her with an affronted look. "Well, sorry for wanting to go out," she said.

Her mother smiled at her, embracing her with a hug. Melanie didn't hug back. She was always like this.

"I'm just trying to help you dear. This is for your own good," she said.

"If you cared, you'd let me live my own life," Melanie muttered.

"What was that?"

"Nothing," Melanie said, pulling away. She went up to her room, working a little bit on the online course she was taking to get a degree. It was something she started out of frustration one day. It was for a nursing certification, and introducing her to the medical, and it was to get certified as a nurse in order to go into that field.

She liked helping others. Being a nurse seemed like something she'd enjoy, and she loved the school. She couldn't wait to get out of this shitty lot situation and go head toward that goal. But, even then she was a little worried a little about it. However, Melanie she did have dreams, and it they wasn't just to be about modeling, that's for sure.

The next day, Melanie woke up and texted Bailey, saying that she would be ready whenever. Bailey responded immediately after, telling Melanie that they could meet up in the early afternoon after her workout. Melanie was shocked that Bailey was working out and skating with her. It was amazing to behold.

When it was time, Melanie went to the door. She looked at her mother, who was in her office.

"I'm going out. See you in a bit," she said.

"All right. Have fun," she muttered.

Melanie could tell her mother wasn't happy, but it wasn't like she would stop her. Melanie walked out, closing the door and sighing.

What now? Melanie wondered what might happen next, or even what she should do. There were many questions she had, but when she got to the skating rink and saw Bailey there, she smiled.

"There you are," Bailey said.

"Yeah, sorry. It's been a bit hectic on my end. My mom is being overbearing as fuck," she admitted.

That was putting it lightly, but Bailey seemed to understand.

"Well, let's get your mind off it. Together," she said.

She grasped Melanie's hand, and Melanie felt a strange heat zip through her body. They went over to the skating rentals area, and Melanie quickly grabbed the skates for them.

"My treat. Whatever you want, I'll get it for you," she said.

Melanie blushed, but she accepted the offer.

"Thank you," she replied.

After they laced up the skates, Melanie felt Bailey grab her hand, and together, they entered the skating rink. At first, Melanie was awkward, almost falling, but whenever she did, a hand was on her waist, and when she looked up, Bailey was there.

"You good?" Bailey asked.

"Yeah. You're strong. Just like before," she said.

For a moment, Melanie didn't really know how to respond to anything. She was intoxicated by the way Bailey held her, feeling happy about everything that she was experiencing. It made her body ache for more, her heart flutter, and it made her crave even more than she thought that she did.

The duo skated around, and as Bailey held her there, she got to feel the rough, but almost caring touch that Bailey had. It was strange, because usually girls had soft skin and felt dainty, but Bailey had that roughness that made Melanie want to just cuddle up to her and experience that warmth. But then, as they skated around, suddenly Bailey grasped her by the waist, holding her bridal-style in her arms.

"Wah--"

As Bailey held her there, she moved her hands to Bailey's neck, clinging to her for dear life. She was shocked, and a little bit scared, but this was...refreshing in a very strange way. She loved the feeling of this, and as she held onto Bailey, she smelled the scent of lavender on her. It was a strange mix of femininity and masculinity, and for Melanie, it made her feel the strangest urge, and an arousal she didn't understand at all.

She wanted to kiss Bailey.

It was a very different thought. She never really experienced attraction toward anyone, but as Bailey held her there, she felt like a princess, and that Bailey was the knight in shining armor that she loved to have around.

They skated for what seemed to be forever, and she didn't want to let this end. Melanie felt like she was in a different world, and the two of them held hands and skated together just like old times. But, it wasn't like how it was in high school. Back then, the both of them were a little awkward with touching, and she felt a little bit embarrassed every time the two of them would. But, she then started to feel something grow stronger between both of them, and she felt a desire that grew within her to new heights, an attraction that intoxicated her and made her crave more.

When the day was over, they returned the skates, both of them still holding hands. Melanie blushed, and she thought about retracting it, but she didn't want to. It was like she felt that urge within her grow. The touch they shared, the closeness of their bodies, all of that made her feel a strange desire to have more.

She did wonder what it would be like to kiss Bailey. Would her lips be soft, or would they be rough? Melanie did kiss her fair share of guys in the past, but they never felt right. But for some reason, with the closeness of their bodies, and the way that the two of them stayed near one another, she wondered for a brief moment if she should go for it.

Was it right? Would she get rejected right away? She didn't think so, but it embarrassed her to no end.

When they went toward Melanie's car, Bailey looked around. The skating rink was closing, but there was a hot chocolate place nearby.

"Want to go there? I don't feel like parting ways yet," Bailey offered.

"S-sure," Melanie said with a flush.

Bailey smiled, still holding her hand as the two of them made their way over to the hot chocolate shop. Together, they ordered two hot chocolates, both of which were steaming hot. They sat on the bench together, sipping and in a pleasant silence.

It was Melanie who was the first to start the conversation, a blush present on her face.

"It's strange, this almost feels like old times," she admitted.

Bailey looked at her, touching her arm and smiling.

"It is. I've missed this. In truth, I feel like we never really left each other, even though our paths did differ over time. I became a personal trainer, and you're a model. I don't want to lose you, but I'm happy with the time that we share together," Bailey admitted.

Melanie didn't want to lose her either.

"I don't want to go back to modeling. I really don't. I kind of want to stay here with you. If that's okay," Melanie said.

There was a pause, and then, Bailey spoke.

"What do you mean by that? You aren't just saying that cause you missed me, right?" she inquired.

Bailey looked at her, and then, Melanie put her cup down.

"Okay, I'm a bit nervous, but there is something I've wanted to do for the last like hour, and I'm super nervous about this, so bear with me," she said.

Bailey looked at her with surprise and a bit of confusion, but then, Melanie leaned in close, straddling her hips. Bailey's eyes widened, and soon, Melanie met her lips with her own.

The kiss was awkward, and for good reason. This was the first time Melanie ever kissed a girl, and it was the first kiss for her in a long time. The two of them stayed there, brushing their lips together and kissing one another in a soft, sensual manner. For Melanie, this was different for her, but in a strange way, it felt right.

The two of them pulled back, looking at one another and immediately smiling.

"I'm sorry, I've wanted to do that for a long time," she said.

She looked at Bailey, who was shocked. She didn't say anything, but she nodded.

"It's all good. I've wanted that too," she said.

Suddenly, Melanie felt Bailey pull her closer, kissing her passionately, and Melanie sat there again, kissing her. It was such a novel feeling, and she really did enjoy it, but she wondered, what would others say if they knew? What would happen as a result? It bothered her, and it made her fear what would happen next.

They stayed there, and for Melanie, it felt nice. When it got dark, Melanie stood up, flushing.

"I should go. Do you want to spend time together tomorrow?" she asked.

"Sure. We can go to the square and see the Christmas tree. I have clients in the morning until two, but we can go that night," she said.

Melanie nodded. "I'd like that. I'll see you then," she said.

Melanie wanted to leave, mostly because she was slightly confused by how much she enjoyed kissing Bailey. But then, she leaned in once again, giving her a kiss and smiling.

"You're fun to kiss you know. I like the way your lips feel," Melanie said.

Bailey smirked at her, and then, she whispered in her ear.

"If you want, you can feel these lips on other places too," she said with a purr.

Melanie blushed, but she nodded.

"Maybe I can sometime soon," she told Bailey, who was smiling at her.

Melanie felt happy for the first time in a real long time. It was a strange feeling, that's for sure, and she wondered how in the world she managed to feel this way. But, Melanie wanted to feel this again and again, and she loved the way Bailey teased her. She didn't understand her feelings completely, but at the same time, Melanie was quite happy with the results.

She wondered what might happen next. Would the two of them go deeper, and understand one another even more? There were so many questions, so very little answers, but Melanie liked the teasing, she liked the chase, and she couldn't wait for more.

Chapter Five

Bailey couldn't believe it. She kissed Melanie, and it was obvious that Melanie felt the same way.

The fact it was happening like this made Bailey feel so different. She never imagined in a million years that Melanie would like her back. The crush that she harbored for the longest time would finally come true.

Or at least, that's what she hoped.

She left the parking lot and tried to text Melanie, but she didn't really say much. Maybe she was just as nervous as Bailey was, which was understandable. Neither of them ever did this before, and it was obvious that this was new. For Melanie, it probably was the first time she kissed a girl, and for Bailey, it was the first time she kissed the girl that she liked.

She tried dating in the past, which all ended in fucking failure. Bailey always wondered why, but if it was due to Melanie, that would make perfect sense. She never got over her, so maybe that's why dating was never an option for her.

Still though, the fact that they kissed, and the fact that she accepted Bailey's advances that Bailey bestowed to her, made her feel happier than ever before. It made her feel so great, and it definitely was something that she enjoyed more than anything else in this world at the moment.

The next day, Bailey texted Melanie, and she did respond, but it was obvious from the words that Melanie still had a lot of considerations. Which was valid, she probably didn't fully understand her feelings, and Bailey could relate. She just felt giddy, but she wondered if this would work.

When Bailey trained her clients, all of them seemed to be doing well. One of them looked at Bailey at the end of the session and smiled.

"You seem more chipper than usual. Meet a guy you like?" they asked.

"Nope, I'm just doing better. It's refreshing," Bailey said.

She wasn't ready to tell others about the woman she pined for, the one she desired for a long time. Bailey didn't want to call this love. That would infer something deeper. But, it was more of a big crush that wouldn't go away. The client nodded, and Bailey grinned.

"Well I'm happy for you, whatever might be going on. I like seeing you happy," the client said.

"Thank you. I do too," Bailey said.

She never felt this chipper during the holidays, but it was like a new life was breathed into her. After her training, she texted Melanie, and they agreed to meet at the square around six to go see the tree and walk around. It wasn't as cold as it usually was during Christmas, which was great for Bailey, cause she wanted to spend all her time that she could with Melanie.

When Bailey got to the square, donning a black jacket and some leggings, she saw Melanie there in the cutest, pink coat. She immediately flushed as she stared at the beautiful woman, eying her beauty.

"Hey there," Melanie said, giving Bailey the biggest hug. Bailey hugged her back, holding her there for a few moments longer than she thought she would. Melanie pulled back, smiling at her.

"So, you want to see the tree?" she asked.

"Yeah, I'd love that," Bailey admitted.

Melanie wrapped her hands in Bailey's own, and Bailey felt her cling to her hand tightly. Bailey blushed, realizing that Melanie wanted to touch her. She led Bailey over to the tree, and when they got there, Bailey looked up.

This was something she saw so many times, but when she went with Melanie, it created a different feeling within her. The feeling of warmth, the relaxed nature that Melanie had, the touch that they shared, all of this made Bailey feel happy.

"You know, this is the first time I've ever felt happy during the holidays," Bailey admitted.

"Really? But you have a good job, and you seem to have a good head on your shoulders," Melanie replied.

"Yeah, but I didn't have you. Having you around makes me feel...happy. It created a happiness I normally don't feel, and it's nice to experience this. I love it,' Bailey said.

She touched Melanie's hand, squeezing it, and she pulled Melanie close. The blonde gasped as Bailey held her there, feeling happy and satisfied.

"You're really happy, aren't you?" Melanie said.

"I am. Honestly, there are a few things I wanted to tell you, but I've been afraid to. If you want, we can talk about it later though. For now, I'm fine with just holding you there, and well, experiencing the moment," Bailey said.

She knew Melanie wanted those answers eventually, but for now, Bailey just wanted to stay close to her. Both of them held one another tightly as they gazed at the beautiful tree. Nobody bothered either of them, and Bailey was glad about that. They took a picture together in front of the tree, and when Bailey looked at it, she smiled.

"I love the way you look here," she admitted.

"Look who's talking. You're gorgeous Bailey," Melanie said.

"I always feel like I look too manly, but when I'm standing next to you, I feel like we look right together," Bailey said.

She didn't really understand why. Maybe it's because it was Melanie, but there was a feeling of happiness that Bailey enjoyed, and a feeling of warmth and desire.

"I feel that same way. I love this. It's a nice little Christmas gift," Melanie said.

"Yeah. Want to go warm up and talk?" Melanie said.

She pointed to the small area where another hot chocolate vendor was. They paid for their drinks, sitting on a bench in the park, lights all around them. Bailey felt so happy, and it was the first time in a very long time that she experienced this type of emotion.

Neither of them said much, but then, Bailey took a deep breath and spoke.

"You know, I've felt this way for a long time," she said.

Melanie looked at her, confusion present on her face.

"What do you mean?"

Bailey wondered if she should tell her, that the feelings she harbored and finally acted upon were feelings she had for years.

"In truth, I never thought you'd like me like this. I always thought you would get together with some guy, and I'd never have a chance. I mean, in high school you were like that, but you'd break up with them shortly after. I just thought it was because of high school relationships. I...I never thought that I had the chance," Bailey said.

Melanie's eyes widened.

"Oh no, I kind of never really felt that same vibe from those guys as I do you," she said.

"I figured. In truth, that night before we graduated I... I almost confessed to you. I wanted to tell you that I had a lot of feelings for you, that I... I've fallen for you, and I know that my confidence isn't the best, but I'm reaching for this. I'm going to be honest with myself, even though expected rejection. When you went off to model, I figured that it was just the end, that I'd never see you, ever again. I took it as such, and I tried to date other girls, but it wasn't the same. None of them were you," Bailey admitted.

She saw the flush on Melanie's face, and then suddenly, she nodded.

"Maybe that's what I've been feeling too. Honestly, all the guys I dated before never made me feel like you make me feel. I've never kissed a girl up until before today. Honestly, for the longest time, I thought I was straight, just asexual cause I never felt that urge to go for anyone. But, when I'm around you...I feel things. When I saw you the first night, I honestly thought you were super-hot. Your muscles are so nice, and I love the way you hold me. You're like the perfect mixture of femininity feminine and masculinity masculine, and I find that it is the hottest thing and I... I really like you, too," Melanie said.

As Bailey heard those words, she grew red as a tomato.

"So, this isn't just a temporary thing. You really do want me, don't you?" she asked Melanie.

She wanted to hear it straight from her. It was then when Melanie took a deep breath, speaking.

"I know my family wants me to find some guy to fall I love with, but I don't honestly think I can. I think I'm in the right place right now, with you. I'm sticking around because I need the break but...I'm hesitant about going back to modeling. You seem to have it all worked out, and that's something I admire," she said.

Bailey scoffed. She wished she did.

"I don't really. I mean, I'm a great personal trainer, and I've had a lot of success with clients, but I don't personally feel like I've truly gotten what I wanted. A part of it was because of you. But I do worry about our relationship. I don't want us to be some sort of secret thing forever. I know for now, we probably will, but I don't want you to have to continue to work on a dream you don't have anymore. If modeling is like that, that is," Bailey admitted.

She looked at Melanie, and she knew her words hit home. Melanie looked down, sighing in frustration as she heard Bailey utter those words.

"You're right though. I haven't felt the spark that I did in the past regarding modeling for a long time Bailey. It's a strange feeling, to experience this sort of thing, but I'm starting to realize that I don't feel the way I did before. I've been spending more time working on my nursing degree than I have in the past. I feel better about it, and I honestly feel you helped me realize that I could have a better life, where I work on my dreams," Melanie said.

Bailey smiled.

"Honestly, I feel the same way. You've woken me up Melanie. And the fact that you share the same feelings I do is...nice really. I don't feel like I'm pretending anymore," she admitted.

"Yeah. I don't feel like either of us are bullshitting. I mean...when you said those words right before I left I... I wanted it. Really badly. I've never been with a woman before, and if I was to be with one now, it would be you," Melanie said.

Bailey looked at her with widened eyes. She didn't think it would go like this.

"You're sure, right? I don't want you to do something you're not ready for, yet," Bailey said.

She watched as Melanie turned away, turning as red as a tomato. Bailey immediately thought she did something wrong.

"I'm sorry I—"

"No, you're fine Bailey! Trust me, I kind of...really want it. After we parted ways I... I went home and touched myself thinking of you. I really didn't want to say this, and I'm kind of embarrassed, but the thought of you and me was just...really nice. And it felt so good. I normally don't get aroused by something like this, but those words made me crave you. I want you Bailey. I want to experience this with you. I feel like...we are finally getting what we both wanted deep down, five years ago. We can figure out the logistics later. Right now, I crave you," Melanie said.

Those words immediately ignited a feeling in Bailey's body. She wanted nothing more than to take her right now, to kiss every inch of her body, and to praise this woman who looked almost ethereal in the light right now. Nobody was around, and soon, she let her hands moved toward her thigh, lightly brushing against the heat that was there. She could feel the heat that Melanie was exuding, and it made her gasp slightly, feeling turned on by the idea of this.

"If you want, we can head back to my place. I don't really think where you're staying is the correct option," she said.

"No. not at all. let's go," Melanie insisted.

She stood up, wrapping her hand in Bailey's own, looking at her. But then, instead of leaving, Melanie kissed her, and the two of them were locked in an embrace. Bailey noticed her lips were desperate, and as they kissed Bailey, she couldn't help but kiss her back. The two of them let their bodies move closer, their lips mingling and intertwining as they did this. For Bailey, she felt like she was experiencing a tiny little part of heaven, and that Melanie was the one who caused all of this.

She noticed Melanie pull away, the obvious blush on her face there.

"Let's...go back," she insisted.

Bailey smiled, seeing the embarrassed look on her face.

"Don't worry, I'll be gentle for your first time," she said.

"Thanks," Melanie said. She twisted her hand into Bailey's own, holding it there, and Bailey began to realize it was a security foe Melanie to do that. She felt happy, and strong when her hand was in Bailey's own. Bailey felt an aura of confidence when she realized this, a feeling of well-being exuding from her.

They walked over to Bailey's car, and soon, they drove back to her place. When they got there, Bailey walked out, smiling at Melanie who simply followed her. When they got to the apartment, Melanie looked at the place, and Bailey could see her eyes widening.

"Your place is huge!" she said.

"Yeah, and a bit lonely. But, it won't be tonight," she said.

She helped Melanie get out of her jacket, and she put her own on the coat rack. She noticed Melanie looking at her thick, muscular frame, blushing.

"You ready?" Bailey asked.

"Yes," Melanie said.

It was then when Bailey pushed her lightly against the wall, pulling her chin up to meet her own. The two of them locked eyes, making Bailey feel the craving for more. It was then when Bailey pressed her lips to Melanie's own, the heat of desire growing within her, and the aching need making her feel stronger than ever before.

Chapter Six

The kiss the two shared was something that shocked Melanie to the core. She loved the feeling of Baileys' lips against her own. At first, the kiss was soft and sensual, but then there was that heat of desperation as the two of them let their lips dance against one another, and the heat of their own aching needs growing even more than they imagined.

Bailey moaned against her lips, and soon, she pushed her tongue forward, meeting Melanie's tongue and letting it dance with it. Melanie immediately started to do the same, both of them fighting for that urge and testing the ability to dominate the other, but Melanie wanted Bailey to take control tonight. She noticed Bailey's hands moved down wards toward her waist, cupping her hips and letting her own grind against Melanie's. The sensation of this immediately aroused Melanie, who moaned against her lips as the two of them let their hips lightly collide. The sensation of this, the small touches that they both shared, the excitement that grew within her, everything was driving Bailey to that point of madness that Melanie wanted to exp9erience. She had never been this horny for a girl before, and the fact that Bailey wanted to pleasure her, turned her on in ways she never imagined.

Bailey grasped her body, holding her hips and cupping her butt. She pulled Melanie into her arms, which shocked the blonde. Melanie clung to Bailey, and in truth, she loved this more than she cared to admit. She noticed that Bailey was so strong, and lifted Melanie like it was nothing, which was a huge turn on. She brought Melanie to the bed, and when they got there, Melanie felt her back hit the soft, white sheets, a blush apparent on her face as she looked at the brunette who was on top of her. Neither of them said anything for a second, just locking locked eyes and letting the tension brew as they gazed upon each other.

Melanie shivered as Bailey kissed down her neck, the smallest of touches enticing her, turning her on and making her beg for more. Her body ached, her pussy quivered with delight, and as she felt each of those little touches, Melanie wondered if fate was just being cruel to her, or if this was real. She noticed that Bailey was smiling as she looked at Melanie's shivering body, lightly grazing her fingers against her.

"You're enjoying this a lot, aren't you?" she said.

"Y-yes," she whimpered with delight.

Bailey smiled, then started to bite down on Melanie's neck, causing the blonde to shiver and cry out loud. Melanie felt her composure start begin to slowly lose control and she knew for a fact that Bailey was enjoying the sounds that she uttered. E time she moved downwards, she continued to tease and caress her flesh, causing Melanie to groan in pleasure.

She felt Bailey lift the sweater that she wore, taking it off slowly to reveal a small black bra. Her Bailey hands draped dragged over her Melanie's flesh, caressing her torso and making Melanie shiver with delight. She groaned at the sensation of Bailey doing this, craving more and more of her sweet touch. The way her lips felt as she kissed down her body, the way that she slowly but surely teased every single part of her, everything was making Melanie's body stand on end, and her desire grew, aching.

She watched as Bailey's lips moved down her chest, touching and teasing the sides of her breasts. Bailey moved her hands to the back of Melanie's bra, taking it off like she'd done it a million times. Melanie gasped as the cold air hit her flesh, causing her nipples to stand on end, and it was only a matter of time before she felt Bailey there, letting her lips move down toward one of the nipples and teasing the very flesh that was there. Immediately, Melanie gasped, holding onto her for dear life as Bailey continued to tease and play with her nipples like it was nothing. Bailey was so skillful, and each of the little touches, the way her lips and tongue moved over the perked perky bud like she was a masterful artist, and the cries that Melanie uttered as she teased her small tits, seemed to turn her on even further. Melanie could tell that Bailey was enjoying this, feeling the rush of pleasure herself, as she continued to dote over Melanie.

But, she soon moved downwards, and Melanie could feel her lips caressing her stomach until they got to the small V-line. She moved her hands toward Melanie's pants, and after Melanie felt her struggle for a brief second, she slipped them off. Melanie watched as her area was exposed, her shaven flesh for her to see.

Melanie blushed, feeling exposed to the one woman she cared about, but then, Bailey smiled.

"You ready?" she asked.

Melanie nodded. Bailey was going to take her tonight, and she wasn't going to let anything stop her.

"Y-yes. I want this," she said.

"I can tell. You're already so ready for me," Bailey said, letting her hands dance against her folds. Immediately, Melanie groaned, suddenly feeling completely exposed because of this woman's touches. Every single motion was enough to drive Melanie to the point of madness, and every time that Bailey did this, she clamored for more. She watched as Bailey moved her apart, letting her tongue tease her folds, playing with the flesh, and enjoying everything about it.

Melanie moaned small sounds as she felt Bailey continue to tease and play with her like no other. Bailey was so good, and when she touched her small sweet spot, immediately Melanie let out a series of small, almost inaudible cries. She felt like a princess, being served by a beautiful queen, and for Melanie, she was in heaven as she felt everything that Bailey did to her. Everything she bestowed to Melanie felt amazing, and although she was certainly not used to these feelings, they weren't bad, that's for sure.

They were novel, and Melanie loved everything about it.

Melanie continued to pleasure her, but then something happened. She felt her touch a spot again, causing her to immediately tense up, crying out in pleasure, and bucking her hips with delight. Everything about this was perfect, and she loved everything that was going on.

She felt her orgasm come on quickly, and suddenly, Melanie clung to Bailey, screaming out in rapturous pleasure as Bailey finished using her lips to tease her, pulling back and licking her lisp, smiling in satisfaction.

"You enjoy that?"

Melanie nodded, her brain unable to form words just yet.

"Good, because I have more where that came from," she said to Melanie with a purr.

Melanie had no idea what this woman had in store for her, but she moved back, grasping something from the nightstand. It looked like a double-sided dildo, ; and she could see the one thick head of it, and blushing blushed profusely. She couldn't remember the last time she had something that big inside of her, but she wanted to be connected to Bailey in this fashion. Bailey quickly lubed it up, pushing one of the sides of the dildo into herself before lubing the other side, spreading Melanie apart, and slowly sliding it in.

Melanie's face contorted with the slight pain. She definitely was not used to the feeling of something inside of her, and for a second, it was extremely uncomfortable. But then, Bailey began to push inside of her and stroke deeper, breaking through that tightness and getting all the way in. Melanie cried out, but then Bailey pressed her lips to Melanie's, silencing Melanie her with a kiss. It did help with the pain, that's for sure, and when Bailey pulled back, she simply smiled.

"You good?" she inquired.

"Yeah. I'm good," she replied.

"You're certainly not used to this, are you?" she teased.

Melanie blushed. "No. This is nice though. I like feeling connected with you inside me," she said.

It probably sounded super stupid, but she certainly didn't mind saying it. She watched as Bailey smiled, then kissed her once again.

"Then let me take care of you," she told Melanie with a purr.

With those words, she started to thrust in and out of Melanie slowly, and Melanie clung to her, crying out in pleasure as she felt her join their bodies together. Bailey felt so good, and the thrusts that she used were perfect in terms of pace. She held onto her for dear life, enjoying the nature of their actions, completely intoxicated in the feeling of movement that Bailey gave to her.

Bailey was moving in and out of her faster and faster, the thrusts amazing and almost too good to be true. She then held Melanie's hips, thrusting in deep, and Melanie cried out. Bailey held onto one of the hips, as Melanie felt her a hand drape against Melanie's press against clit. When she Bailey did that, rubbing it while she thrusted, it was all over.

As Melanie came, she felt like everything was going to just go blank at that any moment. It was so amazing, so intoxicating, and she couldn't really believe that this was happening this way. After she felt Bailey finishing herself, letting out a cry and cumming against her, then she pulled back. Bailey put the toy off to the side, and moved toward the bed.

"You look happy?" she said.

Melanie was. This was the first time she truly did feel happy.

"I do. I want to be like this. I truly, honestly do," she said.

"I feel the same way. I finally got to touch you, taste you, to feel you. It's something I've dreamed of, something I've thought long and hard about for such a long time that finally getting that dream fulfilled...it's nice," Bailey said.

Melanie blushed. She understood how Bailey felt.

"I think it's a little different for me, because it's an awakening of my feelings, but I do appreciate it.

"Yeah. you're not just another conquest, not someone I don't see myself being with Melanie. In truth it's...relieving, to finally get to touch you, and to experience this feeling with you," Bailey said, letting her arms caress Melanie's own. Melanie loved the touch, feeling the excitement grow within her.

"I'm glad. I truly am," Melanie said.

Bailey reached in, cupping Melanie's face. The distance between them was almost nothing, and as Melanie looked into Bailey's eyes, she saw the seriousness of her face.

"Listen Mel. I'm here for you. I...I want to be there for you. Everything about this was a dream come true, and it's a feeling I never want to forget. Don't let me forget it. Please," she clamored.

Melanie nodded, smiling at the brunette, seeing the dedication in her eyes, and the seriousness of her voice.

"I'll make sure you never forget babe."

She kissed Bailey, who smiled at her with a soft smirk.

"Thank you Mel. I believe you. We should sleep though, you look exhausted," Bailey pointed out.

Melanie nodded. She was tired. Plus, she had a lot of questions about her future. She really didn't know what to do. She felt as if she had a battle that she needed to win, and she wanted to finally prove to her family that she was strong enough to do what she wanted in life. But for now, sleep was the primary factor in her life.

"Yeah. We should. Night."

She cuddled up next to Bailey, who was smiling as she moved in close. She felt Baileys' warm arms wrap around her, and everything just felt so right. She wondered if they could be like this forever, and if she would finally have the guts to tell her parents how she felt.

Chapter Seven

When Bailey woke the next day, she saw that Melanie was clinging to her for dear life. It felt nice, especially since she enjoyed the closeness. Bailey wanted it to be like this forever.

Would it be though?

She knew Melanie had a family that wasn't super supportive of her going against the grain. She certainly wished that Melanie would do something about it. It definitely was making her feel like they could never truly be together.

Could they?

Bailey wondered these things, but for now, she wanted to embrace Melanie and hold her close. After a little bit, she noticed Melanie yawning, and Bailey smiled.

"Someone slept well," she teased.

"Yeah, you're comfy to lay on," she admitted.

"Why thank you. So, you enjoyed it then?" Bailey asked.

Melanie blushed, and Bailey thought it was the cutest thing.

"I-I did. But, I'm worried about us. I don't know what to do. If my family found out about you, I'd be fucked," she admitted.

That was the one problem that Bailey had.

"You're going to need to stand up to your family Melanie. I know that it's scary. I mean, I've done it, and I know it's hard, but you have to be stronger. Though, I feel I could've done it in a better way," she admitted.

"But you're living your dream. I'm not. I hate that I'm doing something I dislike so much," she said.

"It's okay Mel. Trust me, I feel the urge to say something to my parents. But I worry too."

"But you're doing so well. Why don't you just tell them?" Melanie asked.

What she didn't know, was that when Bailey finally stood up for herself, her parents called her the worst names out there.

"Because my family hurt me in a lots of ways. I just...I fear making it up to with them. I mean, I know that they don't approve of me doing something other than the family business, and they also are homophobic, so I'm worried about it. But, I'm an adult, and I can do what I want, so there is that," Bailey said.

She was an adult, so maybe that was what she needed to realize. She needed to understand she could accomplish whatever she wanted, with just a little push.

"I think we both need to work through this," Melanie said.

"Yeah, but we have each other. I kind of want to try, but I'm worried," Bailey said.

"You're strong. Trust me on this," Melanie said.

Bailey was strong, but that was a part of the problem. She wasn't used to pressing forward and standing up for herself. But, when she got up, she dropped Melanie off at her car, and made her way to her gym. However, when she got there, she saw someone she thought that she would never see again.

Was this some cruel trick fate was playing? For Bailey, she believed so, but she also didn't really know what else to do about it. She looked at the woman that was there, anger present on her face, but she had to maintain her professional aura.

"Mom," she stated.

"Hi Bailey. I wanted to see you. I figured we could try to work this out. I heard you were training here, and while, I don't really feel the urge to support this, I do want to come in and see you. The truth is, I need some help," her mother said.

Bailey looked at the woman, the person that who didn't want to have anything to do with her for five years. How could she be like this?

"So, you're going to try to make amends after all this time? After you just tossed me away when I said I wouldn't work for Dad's company?" Bailey snapped.

Her mother sighed. "Bailey, it's bigger than that. I'm sorry for snapping at you all those years ago, but you have to realize you put your father and I in a very awkward place. We wanted to make it right for you, and we wanted you to succeed with the company, but it's obvious you didn't want to do that. I want to try to make amends again, to start over; especially since I messed up the first time," she admitted.

Bailey wanted to tell her to go away and never come back, but it would ruin her image as a personal trainer. She knew her father was powerful, so she had to work with her mother, even if she disliked her.

"All right, Mom. I'll do it. Let's get started," she said.

"I'll pay and everything. Plus, I do need the help. I found out from my doctor that if I don't see a trainer and fix my habits soon, I'm going to get diabetes, and put myself at risk for heart disease and the like. I'm just trying to watch out for myself," she said.

"I know. I wish you watched out for your daughter a bit better, like when she decided to make a change in her life," Bailey muttered.

"Sorry," she said.

Bailey signed her up, and although she was not a fan of this, she thought about Melanie. If she could make amends with her mother, then Melanie could as well.

"All right, first and foremost, let's check everything to see where you stand in terms of health and establish a goal," Bailey said.

Her mother nodded, standing on the scale. Bailey looked at all of the measurements, and the doctoral doctor's report.

"Mom, you don't realize how bad your risk for diabetes is, right?"

She shook her head.

Bailey sighed, looking at her.

"Well, I'm going to say although it's the holidays, you definitely need to change this around. I indulge on at Christmas, but you're not going to have a long life if you keep this up. Did something happen?" Bailey asked.

Normally, her mother had it together, and she used to eat healthy, but then, she sighed.

"It's your father. He...fell and I've been taking care of him since. It's been stressful dear, and I've been working on the family business. I wanted to come here to ask if you could help, but I know that's foolish," she uttered.

Bailey felt annoyed by those words.

"So, you didn't come here to better your life? You just wanted to pull me back," she snapped

"No, that's not true dear! I wanted to make amends, to apologize for my treatment of you. If you can help me, please do so. But, I'm sorry that I'm such a mess," she said.

Bailey knew that her mother wasn't going to leave this place until she accepted the apology, and Bailey sighed.

"I won't fully forgive you, because both you and Father said a lot of ugly things, but we can begin personal training. We have a few weeks till Christmas, and if you come in and work with me, we can establish a good regimen to help you," Bailey said.

She was still shocked her mother even thought about coming here, but she was paying for it.

"Thank you dear. And hopefully, we can work to make this relationship right for both of us," she said.

Bailey didn't think so, but she wouldn't tell her mother that. In truth, she had already given up on her, and didn't think that it would become anything bigger more than just a client and -trainer relationship, . but Bailey did have that a small spark of hope, and as she worked with her mother, deep down, she wanted more than anything to have that relationship once again., to have She wanted her mother to work with her and create a life that they wanted to share.

Chapter Eight

When Melanie got to her car, she opened her phone. She cringed at the laundry list of messages from her mother, demanding where she was and why she didn't come home. She sighed, realizing the truth of her lot. She had a crazy mother who wanted nothing more than to harass her like crazy because she didn't come home.

She feared this might happen. Now she would have to go back and try to work things out with her. Already, she was dreading it.

She drove back to her mom's place, and when she walked inside, she heard quick footsteps as they came closer. She looked at her mother, who had a frown on her face, annoyance obvious in her eyes.

"And just, where were you?" she uttered.

"I was with a friend. We went out," she said.

"You could at least tell me," she said.

"You could at least learn that your daughter isn't a fucking child anymore, and doesn't need to be babysat," Melanie muttered.

Her mother looked at her with an affronted glare, her eyes widened, and she winced slightly.

"You dare use that tone with me?" she asked.

"Yes, because I'm sick of you trying to control every goddamn aspect of my life! Let me live," she stated.

"You're under my care, under my roof for the next couple weeks, and you must realize that you're working on your dreams with my help. Your father and I put so much into your modeling, and I'm worried that whoever you're seeing is just creating a bad influence on you," she said.

Melanie didn't think that, in fact, she felt like Bailey was the influence she needed. She helped her figure out things, and in truth, she felt less scared to stand up to her mother, and instead be honest with herself. If anything, this was a blessing.

"Well to be honest mom, she's been a huge factor in my life. She wanted to hang out with me, since the two of us haven't spent a ton of time together. I had a blast, and if you don't understand my own happiness, I don't really know what to do with you," Melanie said.

Her mother scoffed. "Don't tell me you're planning on leaving modeling. I have a gig for you this afternoon," she said.

"Wait, you planned a gig?" Melanie asked, both shocked and angry by those words.

"Of course. You need to keep up your appearances dear, even if you don't like doing them. You will have to get ready so0on, since it is a holiday commercial, and you'll be starring in it," she said.

Melanie wanted to do anything but this. She didn't want to star in some stupid stupid-ass commercial that she would hate. But, she feared standing up to her mom.

"Fine," she said.

"Good dear. See, you've got so much potential. You're beautiful, and you're living a dream I wish I could have had," she said.

Melanie stiffened at those words. Was this really her mother's dream? It would make perfect sense if so.

"Wait, so you've always wanted to be a model?" she inquired.

"Of course. You really didn't figure that out?" her mother replied.

Melanie felt sick to her stomach when she heard those words. She couldn't believe she'd been living such a sham of a life.

"I can't believe you," she said.

"Well, you either do the gig, or go out on the street. Your call," she said.

Melanie didn't have any other options, so she simply nodded.

"Fine," she muttered.

"See, it's that simple dear," she said.

Melanie didn't think it was, but she got ready. Her mother drove her to the studio. When Melanie arrived, she immediately saw the side side-eyes from all of the girls.

She didn't think she belonged here. It wasn't the atmosphere she wanted to be around. All the girls were mean, they all seemed miserable, and there was something about this that made Melanie feel disgusted with herself. But her mother was there. As Melanie got ready, one of the girls looked at her and scoffed.

"You don't belong here," she said.

"And what makes you think that?" Melanie retorted.

"I can see it in your eyes. You're not happy being here. You're ready to quit. I wish I could quit myself," the girl said.

Melanie looked at the redhead, someone who she thought hated her, but there was a look of complete sadness in her eyes.

"What do you mean?" she asked.

"You have a chance to leave, don't you? I don't have that. I only have modeling, and this world is too cold. I'm Rayne by the way," she said.

"Melanie. And you want to quit too, huh?"

"Yeah. I don't like this atmosphere, but I never got a job anywhere else, and I'm scared to leave," she said.

"I feel you. I've been studying to become a nurse but... I have to go through her first," Melanie said, nodding toward her mother sitting with a frown on her face. She was probably still pissed about what their talk.

"It's okay. Least you have some support."

"But if I don't do what she says, she's going to kick me out. She said so," Melanie said.

"I know. But, I think you'll find the strength to tell her, and I think it'll work out for you. I hope it does. I hate working in this line of work, but I'm trapped because this is where I make good money. I don't have some degree to fall back on, so I gotta take what I can get. All the girls here glare at me because I'm one of the more popular models for this type of thing, but deep down, I think they're hurting as well," she admitted.

For Melanie, hearing those words sparked something within, an understanding of sorts about what was going on.

"Maybe they do get it. I never thought of it like that," she said.

"Most don't. Most of us are too scared to think like that, but I can tell from the look in your eyes that you want to live a better, more rewarding life, and this is the way to do it. Standing up for yourself is good, and I hope you have someone who helps you find the strength do so.

Melanie hoped this as well. She thought about Bailey, and although the muscular woman fought her own issues and had her own turmoil, she seemed to be strong enough to help her. Maybe she needed to see her once again. Melanie finished getting ready, and soon, shooting began.

It was the same as it always was, but since hearing Rayne's words, she noticed that the other girls weren't all that happy either. Maybe they were thrown into this as well. Once it was over, Melanie got dressed, and her mother was right outside the dressing room.

"Good job, sweetie! I'll take you out for dinner," she said.

"You don't have to, Mom," she said.

"Nonsense, you did well and followed my instructions, and the photographer's instructions as well. So, you do need to be aptly rewarded," she said.

Melanie didn't think she deserved it, but she followed her mom to the car. She drove them to some popular restaurant her mother loved. When they sat down, Melanie was trying her hardest not to just spit everything out, but then, her mother spoke.

"So dear, you like modeling, don't you?" she asked.

Melanie felt like this was a loaded question, where if she said no, her mother would give her hell and then some, but if she said yes, she wouldn't be true to herself.

"What if I say no? You're living your dream through me, not because I really want to," she said.

"Well, what do you plan to do about it? You can't get a better job. You've been doing this your entire life. Ever since you were young you did gigs, you just got even more popular when you became an adult,' " she stated.

Melanie knew this, that's for sure. She knew for a fact that her mother was definitely pushing it, all throughout her life, and she hated it.

"Mom, I don't want to do this forever. I want to be a better person, and I want to follow my own dreams and passions. I'll continue for now, but you have to respect my choices in life," she stated.

Her mother paused, looking at her with a disdainful glance.

"Are you sure about that? You know that if you have other passions, they'll typically try to overtake modeling," she stated.

"I know Mother. But, I want to be happy. I'll continue for now, but I honestly also want to work on other passions things too. If that's okay," Melanie said.

She knew that it was a contest between trying to convince her mother to leave her alone, and also to appease her, so maybe this might work. After a bit, she finally sighed, knowing that Melanie was right.

"Fine. You can work on other things, just don't forget where you came from," she said to Melanie.

Melanie was happy she at least got some agreement from her mom, even though it was obvious she wouldn't fully agree to what she wanted. But, for Melanie, she knew that this was a start. While she wouldn't dare tell her mom about her relationship with Bailey just yet, she felt that it was the setup for a decent experience, and she would figure out the kinks within it later.

It was a start, but she definitely wasn't ready yet.

Chapter Nine

The next day, Bailey handled some a personal training sessions with a few clients, one of them being her mom. She felt like there was a lot of tension there still, but her mother was trying, and she seemed willing to learn. Bailey was happy about that, but there were still too many questions, and not nearly enough answers.

She didn't get why her mother was seeking her out now. In truth, she still felt her mother hated her, but she was coming in for her sessions, right on time, and it made her realize that there might be more to this than she thought. Maybe her mom really is was willing to work things out.

But she didn't want to get her hopes up. After a bit, she finished with her day, and was about to head out and see if Melanie wanted to hang out. It had been a few days, but then, she noticed something on the screen.

It was a Christmas commercial, yes, but that wasn't what bothered her. What bothered her was the person in it.

"Melanie?" she muttered to herself.

That was the last person she wanted to see in a commercial. She thought she was trying to give up that life, but here Melanie was, working her magic in a commercial. But Bailey could tell that she was miserable. It was obvious in her body language. The redhead was the same.

"I can't believe this. She's letting her mom walk all over her again," she muttered to herself.

Bailey needed to talk to her, so she grabbed her phone and dialing dialed Melanie's number. She heard the sound of the phone ringing, and then, she Melanie picked up.

"Hey Bailey. What's up?" she said.

"Hey. So, we have to talk. Are you free right now?" she inquired.

She hoped to God that she was. There was a pause, and she heard the sound of rummaging items, and then, she sighed.

"Yeah. I am. Let me just tell my mom I'm heading out," she said.

"Come on Melanie. You're a grown-ass adult. She can deal with you being gone for a bit," she said.

There was a pause, and then, Melanie spoke to her.

"You saw it, didn't you?" she asked.

"Yeah, I did, and I want to talk to you. I'm not mad, but something needs to give," she uttered.

There was another pause, and Bailey was about to scream. She couldn't believe that Melanie was doing this.

"Yeah. Let's talk."

The phone call ended after Bailey Melanie told her where she wanted to meet up. Bailey sat in her chair, sighing. She couldn't believe that Melanie was giving into her mother like this, but she would get to the bottom of why she did this.

After she finished getting dressed, she headed out to where Melanie wanted to meet up. She felt the frustration grow within her, the anger starting to come forward. She didn't want Melanie to just give into her mother's desires.

When she got there, she noticed Melanie was already in the corner. For a second, Bailey felt angry, but then she walked over to Melanie with a smile.

"You okay?" she inquired.

"Yeah. Are you though? You seemed pissed over the phone," she admitted.

Bailey was upset, but when she was around Melanie, it seemed to dissipate so easily.

"I am mad, but not at you. So how did it happen like this? You working with your mom and modeling and shit? I saw the commercial, and you looked like you hated it," she said.

"I... I was forced to Bailey. I'm sorry, but I couldn't stand up to her. I told her though, that I want to live my own life. I want to pursue other interests. She doesn't believe in me, but I want to do it," she admitted.

"I know dear. But, you looked miserable. I'm sure nobody else saw it, but I saw it. The other girl did as well," Bailey pointed out.

There was a pause, and suddenly, Melanie sighed.

"Yeah, her name is Rayne. She's someone I've recently started working with. She's in a similar boat. I want to show her that it's possible to get out of this, but I'm afraid of what might happen to me. There's a lot that I don't know, and a lot that I'm very confused about, so I'm trying really hard to figure it out for myself," she said.

"I know. You need to start standing up for yourself. I don't know how many times I have to tell you, but you gotta dear. I know that you're worried about doing so, because well, she's your mom and kind of a bitch. But you're going to continue to be miserable fi if you don't, and that's something I don't want to see. I don't want you to lose yourself. , To in the dreams of another," Bailey said.

Immediately, Melanie looked at Bailey with shocked eyes.

"Wait, you figured out it was her dream?" she asked.

"Of course. You really thought that I didn't notice that Melanie? The reason you follow through with this, is because you refuse to disappoint your mom. You care too much about her to do so, and you know that this is her dream. But, you can't keep living like this forever my dear. You're going to hate yourself if you do. So, quit the act, cut the crap, and start living for you," Bailey insisted.

She knew she was forceful, and probably a bit bitchy. She didn't mean to sound like that, but she was tired of Melanie looking upset. Melanie looked at her, touching her hand and smiling.

"Thank you. You are always here to kick my ass and get me to realize you're right," she said.

"Of course. I mean, I care about you a lot. And if you ever need a place to go, or some place for you to just lay low for a bit, you can always come with me. If you need a place to live, you're more than welcome," Bailey said.

She couldn't believe she was saying this, but she felt that it was necessary. Melanie nodded, looking at her.

"Thank you. I think I may take you up on that, once I've got my life sorted out. What about you though? Have things been better for you?" she asked.

Bailey wondered what in the world she should tell Melanie. She wanted to explain to Melanie that she and her mom were on better terms, but she was still worried about taking this chance.

"Honestly, my mom and I met up. I'm helping her, but, I still feel like it's weird. It's almost wrong of me to do so, after she fucked me over, but I feel that she's starting to understand. I'm trying to work it out, to get my parents to accept me for the mess that I am, and you should too," Bailey said.

She looked at Melanie, who seemed to understand.

"Yeah, I'm trying Bailey. I'm glad that I can rely on you," Melanie said.

"I'm trying to be there for you, but you gotta stand up for yourself. Mel. I've seen you do it once before when we were younger, and you seemed so happy. And it's obvious that you like me, and you want to be with me, so you should buckle down and just be honest with her," Bailey said.

She was probably giving tough love at this point, and maybe sounded like a bitch, but Melanie took it, and she was glad about that.

"Thanks. I'm really trying Bailey. You give me the confidence to do so," she said.

"I'm glad. You should be strong Melanie. If you do that, then we can work out our future together. Because... I want you to be in my future, but I know that I can't ask for that immediately, but you have to work through the kinks yourself.," she explained.

The blonde nodded, understanding her words.

"You... really do care, don't you?"

"More than you know Melanie. You don't understand, I care so much about you that you don't realize just what I would do for you. I care about you a lot, and I know for a fact it's hard out there, but you got this, and you have me, who will be there for you no matter what?" Bailey said.

Nobody in the area was paying attention, so she stole a kiss from Melanie, who blushed.

"Thank you, Bailey. I feel the same way. You make me feel like it's worth it to stand up for myself," she replied.

"Good. Because I want to make sure you feel worth it. I want to show you that life is worth living, and that you don't need to live in the shadow of your mother all the time," she admitted.

She knew that it wouldn't be easy for her, but Bailey believed in her lover. Melanie got up, and the two of them held hands.

"Want to go for a walk? We can go shopping too," she said.

"Fine by me," Bailey said.

The duo walked, holding hands and laughing. Bailey wanted to stay like this forever. They shopped, bought each other gifts, and it was the most perfect date in Bailey's eyes. At the end of it, they went back to the car, and Melanie looked at Bailey with a gaze that was unwavering.

"Thank you," she said.

"You're welcome. You mean a lot to me, Mel," Bailey said.

"You do too. I feel like... you're the piece of the puzzle that's been missing, that one little push that I needed in life. So, thanks," she replied.

They shared a kiss, and as Bailey pulled away, she felt those words at the tip of her tongue. She loved Melanie, and she wanted nothing more than to be there for her, and it was obvious that Melanie felt the same way. But she feared telling her, because their lives were still a little all over the place, so for now she would part ways with a kiss, and they would go from there.

"I'll see you soon," Melanie said.

"Good. Tell her. Be honest with yourself.," Bailey said.

Melanie nodded, and as she went to the car, Bailey hoped more than anything that Melanie would one day take the advice that she gave her.

It would mean the world to her if she did.

Chapter Ten

When Melanie got to the car, she wanted to call her mom and tell her immediately that she was in love with Bailey, and sick of living a line life she didn't even care about. But she held back, knowing deep down that if she told her mom this now, it would spell trouble. So, Melanie went home, going to her computer and researching various aspects of nursing.

It appeared there was a great nursing school in the area. She decided to apply for scholarships, since she probably would need all the help she could get when she finally did tell her mother. She managed to score a little bit of financial aid, but wouldn't hear about the results or her acceptance to that the nursing school until about a week from now, which was right before Christmas.

This gave Melanie time to prepare.

While her mother did bark at the dinner table that she wanted Melanie to keep up with her modeling, and Melanie would try to weasel her way out of it, she was poring over her studies, taking her tests, and working to finish up her basic online education. In order for this to work, she needed to be done super quick, and she felt that urge grow within her.

There was something that felt wrong about this, though. Something that felt ominous in the air.

It was about three days after she submitted everything that she heard it. She was heading downstairs to grab get a bit glass of water, when she heard her mother on the phone talking to someone.

"Yes. She is definitely willing. I want her to travel the world and work with this company. She told me that she does have other interests, but she would have to be a complete dumbass to not work with you. Yes, I get it. She won't have a choice in the matter. I really don't care," she said.

There were some more garbled sounds, and then, Melanie realized the truth of it. She was about to be thrown into a job that she hated, away from Bailey. While she wouldn't mind the travel aspect, the fact that her mother would be there with her the entire time sounded awful, and it stressed her out.

"Fucking shit," she said.

She rushed to her room, checking her applications. Fortunately, the scholarships had started to flood in, but she wouldn't know about the ultimate answer about her acceptance into the school she wanted to until a few more days from now. Melanie prayed for this, but she also wondered how she would break it to her mother.

They were about to fight, that was for sure. Bailey and Melanie wanted to be together, and that's exactly what Melanie desired. She wanted to help others, to live out her dream of being a nurse. But, her mother wanted to groom her into the perfect little model, to continue to achieve beauty standards that she felt were wrong. It all just frustrated her, and she hated that she was going through all of this right before Christmas.

Her mother always had Christmas dinner on Christmas Eve, so the next day they could all just relax. Bailey could come over, and they could spill it then, but Melanie knew that she may might be homeless during for Christmas. She wished more than anything this was all simple to figure out, but it wasn't.

But Bailey was the one that she cared about the most. She pushed her to live her dreams, to finally go for that degree that she wanted. It was refreshing to have that kind of support, and there was something about it that made Melanie happy. She wanted more than anything to live her dreams, but she knew that with each of these dreams, came the crushing reality that she was about to lose someone that supported her.

It was scary, but Melanie kept to herself over the next couple of days. She hoped more than anything, that by some miracle, she didn't end up losing her entire family, and instead, they understood the pain that she went was going through, and supported her. But, as she studied, she also packed a few of her essentials, in the off chance that they didn't. The last thing she wanted to do was to stick around and live with toxic people who didn't let her follow her dreams.

It was a strange situation, one that Melanie didn't really understand. She felt that with time, it would get easier, and the answers would come sooner or later.

Chapter Eleven

Bailey still wasn't used to her mother coming in, but over time, she treated her more like a client than a member of the family. She helped her with treatments, and eventually got used to it. It wasn't like she was happy to have her here, but it was obvious she paid well, so Bailey wouldn't complain.

It was definitely was frustrating having her there and that the elephant in the room bothering her. However, one day after her session, her mother hung around, and Bailey looked at her with concern.

"What's the matter?" she asked.

"I wanted to take you out for dinner sweetie. I think we need to talk," she offered.

Bailey hesitated. She didn't know whether she could trust her mother or not, especially after what she did. But, one look in her mother's eyes told her that her mom wanted to patch things up.

"Are you sure?"

"Yes. I'm sorry if it's a bad time but consider this a gift for being a great trainer," she said.

Bailey hesitated, still sore about what her mom did in the past, but she agreed.

"Sure. Let's go," she said.

She was hesitant about showing any emotion to her mother, but her mom kept quiet for the most part. She motioned to her car, and Bailey hesitated, but got in. If worst worse came to worst, he could always uber back to her gym.

When they got to the restaurant, Bailey realized where her mother was taking her. She looked at the restaurant with surprise, but then, her mother spoke.

"I told you this was a treat," she said.

"Fine."

They were seated; and the atmosphere was tense at best, at worst, stifling. Bailey had no idea what to make of her mother's actions, but instead kept quiet, trying her best to contain her emotions. After the waiter grabbed took their orders, she looked at her mother, waiting for the older woman to talk.

"It's been a while hasn't it," she started.

"Five years. Right after you kicked me out, I had to figure out my own life," she said.

"I know. And that's where I fucked up. I'm here to apologize Bailey. I'm really sorry for the way that I treated you when you were younger. It's just... when you disagreed with working at the company, your father was hurt," her mother started.

Bailey tensed, holding the table and looking at her.

"You realize why I did that, right? Because I wanted to live my own life, pursue my dreams, and be happy," she said.

"I know dear. And that was my fuckup. I realized over time that you were happy doing this. I didn't hear from you, and I assumed that you never wanted to come back, so I didn't reach out. But things got worse over time, and I hated that was the case. Thank you though, for giving me a second chance," she said.

Bailey was trying to be an adult here, really trying to keep her cool, but it was proving to be harder than she imagined.

"You're not going to disown me anymore, right?"

"I'm not. I wanted to apologize Bailey. I wanted to say I'm sorry for ostracizing you. I wanted to say I'm sorry for being the worst parent ever. I know that you're an adult, but I still feel guilty, so I hope that one day, maybe in the future, we can be a family again. I wanted to invite you to Christmas dinner too," she said.

Bailey's eyes widened.

"Like, on Christmas day, dinner?" she hadn't been to a dinner in so long that it sounded unreal.

"Yes. I want you back in our lives. And, if you want to bring someone, let me know," she said.

Bailey nodded. She decided to tell her mom right then and there that she was seeing someone, a girl. She hoped that her mother would take it well.

"I do have someone. Remember Melanie?" Bailey asked.

"That pretty model girl? Of course," her mother said.

"Well, she's been going through a rough patch herself. Her parents are overbearing as piss, and she's trying to get away. I... I like her Mom. More than I thought I would. And I want to bring her to Christmas dinner, fi if that's all right with you," she offered.

She wondered if her mother would agree. It was rare for her to be all right with something like this, but then, her mother beamed at her, and Bailey took that as a good sign.

"Of course. She's more than welcome to come to dinner," her mother said.

Bailey looked at her mother with surprise.

"So, you knew I was gay?"

"I had a feeling considering you never had a boyfriend and were always with her. Which isn't a problem at all. I should've been a better parent toward you. I know how shitty parents can be, and I'm trying really hard. I know that your dad was mad about you choosing a different career, but I told him you've done well and it shouldn't be an issue. He's still a little bit sour about it, but I think seeing you after all this time might help," she offered.

Bailey wondered if that would really work. Would he accept her for the woman that she was now? She was curious, that's for sure.

"Well, I'll show up. I'll be there Christmas day. I think Melanie would love to tag along. She needs support right now, Bailey said.

"You're really helping her, aren't you?" her mother stated.

Bailey nodded. "I like her a lot, but I'm worried that things may go a different way. But I can't hold this back mom. I really can't. I know what I'm feeling is real," she admitted.

"Just say something. You and I both know that you're the type who will beat around the bush in order to avoid the inevitable. You just need to tell her sweetie," her mother said.

Bailey nodded. "Yeah. Thanks, Mom."

"Anytime. I'm working on being a better parent, and you seem to love personal training, so I can't complain. Your father would benefit from this as well," she stated.

"Yeah. I feel that," Bailey replied.

The two talked, it seemed, forever. Bailey realized this was the first time in a long time she had spoken real words to her mother. Her mother seemed to care, and the past issues that were there were soon gone. Bailey wondered what might happen next, but for now, she was just happy that her mother was at least talking to her.

After dinner, her mother drove her back to the gym. When she parked, she looked at Bailey with a smile.

"I'm glad I reached out, you know," she said.

"Are you sure?"

"Yes. You're definitely stronger than before, and honestly, I feel your father will understand you this time around too. We only wanted what's best for you and... I'm proud of you," her mother replied.

Bailey felt her heart skip a beat at those words. She had never heard her mother say that. She was always working on grooming Bailey. But now, hearing her mother say it, made Bailey smile.

"Thank you, Mom. For real. I appreciate everything," she replied.

"Good. I'm glad I can help," her mother said.

They parted ways, and for the first time, in a long time, Bailey felt happy after seeing her mom. She was bitter about the past, but now, she felt better. She was happier than ever before knowing that her mother was doing better, and that they she wanted to repair their broken, family relationship.

However, she had a feeling something was wrong with Melanie. While she didn't know what it was, she called her anyway. The phone went to voicemail . After Bailey left a message asking what was going on, she wondered herself if there was a reason for her actions.

She wondered if the two of them could work out their lives. She had a feeling her debacle issues with her mother would, but there was something eating at Bailey. Something that bothered her regarding about the state of Melanie's family, and she wanted to help in whatever way possible.

Chapter Twelve

Melanie ignored her phone for a few days. It was still a couple of days till Christmas. She felt her heart lurch when she saw the email regarding with her acceptance to the nursing school of her dreams. It was amazing she did got it, but she knew that actually fulfilling her dreams would be the hard part.

She finally turned her phone on, noticing messages from Bailey. She quickly responded with Sorry, had a few issues. We can talk now." After she pressed the send button, she got a quick response back from Bailey. She said she wanted to meet at the park, and while Melanie was fine with that, in her mind she felt slightly worried.

She didn't know what to do. She wanted to be with Bailey, to live her own life, but the fact that her mother was so overbearing made her sick to her stomach. She hated this, wanted nothing more than to figure out a way to get the hell away from her family, but she feared the consequences. But, when she saw Bailey, all the fears somehow went away. However, Bailey looked at her with annoyance.

"Why haven't you been answering my messages?" she asked.

"Sorry Bailey. I've been... going through some shit."

"No shit Sherlock. I wanted to talk to you, if that's okay," Bailey offered.

Melanie could tell from the frown and furrowed brows that Bailey was definitely upset. She also noticed that her eyes were wide, and she seemed tense, but there was some semblance of care there.

Melanie just wanted to break down and cry, but she sighed.

"It's my family. The truth is Bailey, I'm at a crossroads," she explained.

"How so?"

"Well, my family is pushing the modeling shit really hard. I overheard my mom saying that she wanted me to travel the world. I don't want to do that though, not like this. If I were to travel, I feel like I would go with you or something. But, I know that's not possible. She wants to go with me, and she wouldn't allow anyone to come along," Melanie said.

She felt her body collapse next to Bailey, and as she sat there, Bailey touched her hair. The touch felt so good, and she certainly enjoyed it. It made her feel welcome, like she mattered.

"It's okay. You'll get through it," she said.

"I know babe, but I'm worried. I also had a couple other things happen too. I've been working on nursing school too, and I finally got enough scholarships to cover it, so I could go. I also got accepted the other day," Melanie said.

Bailey looked at her with widened eyes, surprise obvious on her face.

"Holy shit. That's amazing!" she cried out.

"Yeah. I'm glad that I did it, but I'm also worried about the future. I really don't know what to do. I want to go to school, I want to tell my mother to fuck off, but I'm scared to do so. I'm definitely at a crossroads," she replied.

She looked at Bailey, who had a smile on her face. How could she be smiling at a time like this. But then, Bailey spoke.

"You and I both had some interesting occurrences it seems," she said.

Melanie looked at her with confusion, unsure of what she meant by that.

"W-what do you mean?"

"What I mean is, both of us have had some major changes with our family since we last saw one another," she explained.

Melanie was definitely unsure what she meant by that, but then, Bailey explained.

"While you weren't talking, I reconnected with my mom. She actually started out as a training client, and I was surprised she even came out to do it. At first, I wasn't all that happy about it, since well, it's her. But I was actually was fine with it after a while," Bailey explained.

Melanie couldn't believe this. She thought that Bailey would never get along with her parents, ever. Mostly because she thought that relationship was over.

"I'm surprised you managed to patch everything up," she stated.

"It took a little bit to accept, but I know that my mom is trying her best, and I know that I should be more supportive. It's hard though," Bailey admitted.

Melanie understood that one. She was more on the receiving end of that type of issue.

"I just wish my family accepted it more. I hate that they don't," Melanie replied.

"Honestly, are they having a Christmas dinner? Let me come over and let me explain it. I'm sure that your mom would be fine if it's just me, and we can make it work," Bailey explained.

Melanie wasn't sure about this. She did tell her mom that she'd been talking to Bailey, and while her mother wasn't encouraging about it, she didn't stop Melanie.

"Okay. I'll do that. I'll discuss it when I get home," she said.

"Good. I want you to tell her that I'm a friend. We will tell them everything. I know it will cause some drama. I don't care. I'm sick of seeing the woman I've fallen for suffering because her family is a bunch of unaccepting assholes," Bailey stated.

Melanie felt her eyes widen at those words. She rarely saw Bailey get that fired up, and there was something strangely hot about it.

"I've never seen you so passionate," she admitted.

"I'm just tired of living a life that isn't for me. I don't want you to go away. I care about you too much. In fact... I love you Melanie. I really do. And I'll do anything to take care of you. If they kick you out, you can live with me. If they don't accept, fuck them. I'll support us, one way or another," Bailey said.

The conviction in her words, the way that Bailey said everything, sparked a fire within Melanie.

"Thank you, Bailey. I owe you everything," she replied.

"You don't owe me shit, Melanie. I'm doing this because I care for you, and because I want to show you what it's like to be cared for. I'm tired of you being kicked around by a bunch of people who really don't care. If they don't care, they don't care, and I'm not going to let it affect me us for the rest of my our lives," Bailey stated.

Melanie nodded, understanding all of this.

"Yeah. I'm sure of it," she said to Bailey.

"Good. I'm glad you're willing to work with me. I know it's hard," Bailey admitted.

"Yeah. I can tell that you're worried about everything as well," Melanie said.

"I mean, I'll be seeing my dad for the first time in a while, and that could be hit or miss. I will say if your family doesn't accept you, mine will. Already talked to my mom, she's cool with you. She knows about us actually. I explained, and she was not surprised, but supportive. Which was nice," she said.

Melanie nodded. "That's good. Thanks Bailey. This was what I needed to hear," she admitted.

"Hey, sometimes you just gotta hear the right thing," Bailey said with a smile.

Melanie intertwined her hand in with Bailey's own, holding it there.

"I got you a present actually," Melanie said.

Bailey looked at her with surprise. Melanie blushed, but then she dug into her pocket.

"I was going to wait until Christmas, but I really wanted to give you this," Melanie said.

Bailey looked at her with confusion, but then, Melanie placed a little box in her hands. Bailey looked at Melanie with confusion, unsure of what to make of this.

"What is this?"

"Just open it."

She nodded, popping open the trinket box and seeing the two bracelets.

"What is this?" she asked.

"It's two bracelets. I know that I've been distant, but I wanted to get you something. So that... no matter what happens, you're thinking of me. Because I care a lot about you," she said.

Bailey felt happiness. She truly did love her, and Melanie thought this was the beginning of a newer, brighter future.

"Thank you, Melanie. This is... the best gift anyone has given me. I'll wear it always and cherish it forever," she said.

"You're here for me, you're going to stick by my side no matter what. I'll be there for you, and I'll stay by you as well," Melanie replied.

Melanie felt Bailey step forward, pressing her lips to Melanie's her own. The two of them kissed, both of them lost in the way that their tongues mingled and touched. Melanie felt true happiness, and she loved more than anything else the desire that she had, and the pleasure that she felt.

After they pulled away, Melanie and Bailey spent the day together. When Melanie got back, her mother looked at her with a quizzical glance.

"Where were you?" she asked.

"I was meeting with Bailey. By the way, is it cool if she comes to dinner tomorrow? She wanted to spend some time with me, and I don't want her to spend the holidays alone," Melanie said.

Her mother looked at Melanie with a wary eye.

"You sure? You never ask to bring people to dinner. What gives?"

How could she explain it? She didn't want to spill everything to her mother yet. She wanted Bailey there to help.

"She wanted to spend the holidays with me. She doesn't speak to her family all that much, so I said if you're cool with it, I'll invite her," Melanie explained.

Her mother pursed her lips, but then, she sighed.

"Fine. But just dinner. We need to discuss your future anyways," she said.

Melanie didn't know what to make of that, whether it be what she heard of before, or something else. But she thanked her mom, although she was far from happy about it. When she texted Bailey explaining the situation, she heard a tone of happiness from the brunette. Melanie was quite happy with the results, but the real test came tomorrow, when they would have to face her family. She would need to stand up for herself in order to follow her dreams.

Chapter Thirteen

Bailey was happy that Melanie's family at least agreed to her coming over, but she wondered if she could convince them to let Melanie live her life. Every time she was around Melanie, she saw a smile on her face, something that warmed her heart and made her happy. Bailey wanted to continue seeing that, she just didn't know how.

She got ready the next day, putting on a blazer and a skirt. She drove to Melanie's address, and when she got there, she texted Melanie that she was outside. She didn't want to go in alone. There was the sound of a door unlocking, and Melanie came out. She was in a beautiful red dress, and when she raced over to Bailey, she smiled.

"Hey. Sorry for being so quiet. I've been a nervous wreck," she stated.

"I really don't blame you. So, do they know?" Bailey asked.

Melanie shook her head.

"My mom thinks that you're just a friend. She's a little concerned but isn't asking questions. Same with my dad," she admitted.

"Well shit! Sounds like we are gonna spill the beans then," she admitted.

"Yeah. I feel that. I'm more worried about how they'll react when I say I don't want to follow her dreams anymore. I want to create my own story, but I'm scared to," Melanie admitted.

Bailey pulled Melanie into her arms, holding her there and stroking her hair.

"We'll make it. We got this. I'll protect you," Bailey said.

She wanted to be there for Melanie, even if she knew that they were about to fight the biggest fight of their lives. She wanted to get Melanie out of that situation, and she wanted her to have a good Christmas. When they walked in, Bailey immediately saw a woman with salt and pepper hair, who was pretty in her prime, but had succumbed to old age a bit.

"You must be Bailey. It's been a while. Lara," she said.

"I remember you Lara. It has been a while. Seems like Sam is doing well too," Bailey said, looking at the older man entering the room. He too looked a little bit distraught, but Lara nodded.

"Yeah, we've been doing well. Trying our hardest to ensure that our daughter gets the best education possible. Sounds like she met up with you by chance," Lara said, eying Bailey. Bailey could tell her mother was not happy to see her. It was obvious this was going to be awkward.

"Yeah well, we grew close again. Plus, it's rare to see her in town, so why not?" Bailey said with a smile.

"Foolish of you to think that you're just going to waltz into someone's home though," she said.

"Your daughter invited me. I'm not waltzing in anywhere. Merry Christmas to you too," Bailey said.

She didn't like this woman, and it was no surprise that Melanie was the way she was. Lara and Bailey certainly didn't get along, and she could tell Melanie saw that, but she didn't say anything.

"I'll have dinner ready in a few. You can stay in the living room," Lara said.

Bailey looked at Melanie, who nodded. They made their to the sofa, turning on the TV, so that it was loud enough to muffle their conversation.

"Your mom is a bitch,' Bailey said.

"Yeah, she's been quite rude all day. It isn't just you, it's everyone. She's been mean to Dad too," Melanie explained.

"Well sounds like someone is totally not in the Christmas spirit and is trying to ruin it for the rest of us," Bailey muttered. She hated those types, and it felt like it was an obligation to be here.

"Well, I feel like she's going to be even worse very soon. You're sure you want to do this, right?" Melanie asked.

"Damn sure."

They talked a little bit, and Bailey could see Lara side-eying her. She didn't like this woman one bit. For some reason, she was worse than when she was in high school. She remembered Lara being overbearing, but not like this.

When dinner was finally served, Bailey felt the air change. There was a tenseness there, but she also could feel the slight relief from Melanie. The duo went to the kitchen, sitting and eating dinner. Sam didn't say much, just looking at his book and sipping some tea.

"Well, this looks good," Bailey said.

"Sure does," Melanie replied.

"I'm glad you'll like it. So, how has life been Bailey?" Lara asked, her voice judgmental as if she was trying to find something to bitch about.

"Well, it's been good. After high school, I ended up going into personal training, and I'm one of the best in town."

"Ahh, so you didn't go to college then. I'm surprised, I thought you'd spend all your time there," she said.

Bailey could hear the malice in her voice from a mile away.

"No, I just got my certification and I got my associate's in marketing. It's worked well for me so far.

"I see. So, I think it's time for me to say something to Melanie especially, but you should know too, since she's your friend," Lara started.

Melanie and Bailey both looked at one another, and Bailey smiled at her with reassurance. She hated that it was going this route, but it had to be done somehow.

"What is it? She's still modeling,' Bailey said.

"Well, I want her to go international. I have a hookup with one of the guysan agent who helped helps international models get big, and he wants her to travel the world. I'll be accompanying her, of course," Lara said, a smug grin on her face.

Bailey looked at Melanie, who was shaking slightly.

"Mom..."

"Come on, this is your dream Melanie. You and I both know that you're not happy just doing the same gigs," she said.

Bailey looked at Melanie, who was struggling to speak.

"I guess it's time for you to hear the news then too," Bailey said.

"Whatever do you mean?"

Bailey grasped Melanie's hand, and she stood up.

Melanie shivered, but Bailey kept a grasp on her hand, trying to reassure her that they would make this work.

"Melanie has told me about her modeling career and why she hates it. It sounds like she's being treated like dirt, instead of like a person. You don't care Lara, and I can could tell from the moment I walked in that you utterly hate me as well," she said.

Lara glared at Melanie.

"She can't do that. She's my daughter."

"And you don't listen. Melanie hasn't felt the desire to model in a long time. She's been working hard, but she doesn't want to do this. She wants to live her own life," Bailey said.

"And how do you know so much about our family affairs? You're not even a part of this," Lara snapped.

"Because, I told Bailey everything. Mom...I don't want to do this. This isn't my dream,' Melanie stated.

Bailey looked at Lara, whose eyes were bulging out of her head.

"What the—"

"You don't care Mom. The truth is, I heard about this conversation a week ago. You were planning this behind my back, and I can't deal with that anymore. I'm tired of you controlling my life!"

There was a silence, and Bailey could see from the anger that seethed emanated from Lara's fact face, that it was the wrong answer.

"You don't know anything, you dumb kid," she stated.

"No Mom, I do. I know that this isn't the life I wanted. I'm not happy. I haven't been for years. You've been throwing this dream on at me for so long, that it took me forever to realize that it isn't mine. But, when I talked to Bailey, and she helped me realize the truth, I... didn't want to go back. I realized this gig job had taken all of the life energy out of me, and I'm suffering from for it. If you really cared Mom, you'd listen," she said.

Her mother looked at Melanie, and the two of them had a glaring contest, almost as if there was that urge to say something, anything that could change it. Then, Lara sighed, looking at Melanie with annoyance.

"So, you're finally betraying me. I knew it would come to this," she muttered.

"Mom, I didn't betray you, you've forced me to live the life of a liar, and I'm sick of lying. I don't want to be a model. This was never my dream. You know whose it was? Yours," Melanie stated.

Lara's eyes bulged, shock obvious on her face.

"How dare you—"

"It's obvious Mom. You've been using me for so long that I feel like I'm getting worse and worse. Bailey helped me, and the truth is mom... I love her. I want to be with her, and I'm happy to have her by my side. She's the support I need, not you with your fake dreams and your pushing for me to succeed. The only reason you're like this right now, is because you don't really care, and you think you can run all over me. I'm done. It's time for me to live my life, and if you can't accept that, I'll leave," Melanie said.

Her mother looked at the duo with a gasp.

"Love her? That means—"

"Yes Mom. I'm gay. This should be obvious. I've never liked guys, I remember you'd pressure me into guys, but I don't like them. You never accepted me for who I was, and you consider me to be nothing more than just someone you pushed out of the womb. I don't think you truly love me Mom, and I'm sure I can prove it. But, I'm not going to let the love that I have , go away. I love her Mom. I'm going to be going to school for to become a nurse. I've been working on signing up for classes under the radar, through the use of different scholarships and such. But, I'm not going to let you continue to tell me that I'm never going to make it, that I have to continue to model for people I utterly hate. I'm just... done Mom," she said.

Her mother looked at Melanie with anger on her face, her body oozing with distaste.

"I can't believe it. You really think you can just leave? After all I've done for you," she stated.

"You didn't do shit for me Mom, besides give me issues with trusting others and trying to figure it out for myself. I know that you don't really care. You're a sham of a person, and I hate that you're like this. I'm done Mom. I'm going to be a nurse., I'm going to stay with this woman, because she makes me happy, something I haven't felt in a long time., and I'm not going to let my past get the best of me. Maybe you should learn to accept your child instead of trying to mold your own bullshit onto me," !" Melanie cried out.

She looked around, noticing that Lara was quite angry, and Bailey could see the setting face that she showed.

"You little shit," Lara said.

"I may be a little shit, but I'm not going to let things get worse from here," Melanie said.

"You're a waste of energy," her mother said.

"And you're a waste of a parent. I've met better parents, ones that accept me for who I am, and ones that won't turn their backs on their kids," Melanie stated.

Her mother looked at her, and then her father.

"What do you think? She's wrong, right? She's just going to make her life worse!" Lara cried out.

Sam looked at the women, and then, he spoke.

"I think she's onto something Lara. I mean, this is the first time you've had to deal with independence. You probably just aren't used to it," he said.

Lara glared at him, and then at Melanie.

"I don't want you in my house anymore. Figure out your own goddamn place to live," she stated.

"Don't worry Mom, I was actually going to tell you that I'm moving out soon. I don't want to be near you, and Bailey is offering me a place to stay. So, I don't need you Mom, and I wish that you'd accept me for who I am and do something about it. I'm sick of this. I'm sick of pretending, and if that you really want to be proud of your daughter," Melanie said.

She got up, glaring at her mother, and then she looked at Bailey. Bailey looked on in disbelief at what just happened.

"You have nobody to blame but yourself, Lara. You hurt your daughter, and you took away her chance at self-expression, so I don't blame you for losing everything. You chose this route, now follow through with it," Bailey said.

"And what do you know about following through anything? She was about to have the world. She was about to become a famous model," Lara cried out.

This brought forth a feeling that Bailey forgot about, something that ate away at her like a bad itch. She smiled to Lara, looking at Melanie's mother with a smug face.

"I know what it's like. I turned away an entire company because I wanted to live my way. I know when it's time for me to choose my battles, and I know when it's also time for me to be honest with myself. And I will say, right now I'm feeling more honest than I have in the past," Bailey said with a smile.

The look on Lara's face was priceless as Bailey got up, turning to Melanie and smiling.

"Grab your stuff. You're coming with me," Bailey told her with a smile on her face, a reassuring glance that said it all.

Melanie looked at her, but Bailey wasn't backing down. She looked at Melanie with a smile, feeling happy about the way things were going. She was ready to face the future, and help Melanie out.

She walked over to the door, and noticed Melanie had grabbed most of her stuff already.

"You were planning on leaving?" Lara asked snidely.

"Mom, I knew you were going to kick me out, so I packed early. I'm not afraid of you. Bailey's taken taking care of me, and I'm happier than ever. I couldn't think of a better person to go with," Melanie said.

"But I raised you. I gave you everything," she cried out.

"You gave me a hellish life, and you made it completely overwhelming. I never wanna come back Mom. Sorry," she muttered.

Melanie trudged out of there, and Bailey walked her to the car. Neither of them said anything for a moment., for tThey were both trying to process what happened. But Bailey was happy about it all., and sShe knew that there was a chance that it would get better from here, and she felt happy about that. They would continue their lives together, no matter what., and Bailey was happy with the way life was going, ready to create a new life, and ready to bring Melanie to a better, less toxic place, so that she could live her own life.

Chapter Fourteen

Melanie didn't say much, still shocked by what just happened. She couldn't believe they had did done this, that the two of them were finally together. She dreamed of having someone who cared about her for so long, and Melanie wondered if there was any way that the two of them could work this out, and have a meaningful life.

Melanie looked at Bailey, who smiled at her, reaching her hand out and squeezing it. Melanie felt happy with the touch, but she wanted to know what would happen next.

"Why did you do it?" she asked.

"Because I wanted to be with you, and I wasn't going to let some shitty person ruin your life anymore Melanie. I know you are better than this, better than her, and I feel like, once you get it together, you'll be much happier than before," Bailey said.

She was right. Melanie already felt happier, and she was certainly ready for whatever life would throw at her.

"Thanks Bailey. You've saved me so many times, I don't even know what to think about that. I know for a fact that you're the best thing to happen to me, and I'm so grateful for you," Melanie said.

"I'm grateful for you as well," Bailey told her with a smile.

When they got to Bailey's place, Melanie felt happy, for the first time in a long time. Bailey just felt perfect, and she didn't know what would happen next, but it was certainly for the best. The two walked into her home. When Bailey turned on the lights, she noticed how beautiful it lit the place.

"It sucks that we had to leave in the middle of dinner, but your mom was being a super bitch, and I just don't have time for that," Bailey admitted.

"I feel the same way," Melanie said.

She sat on the couch, taking all of it in. She felt Bailey's a presence next other, and she noticed that Bailey joined her on the couch. Bailey looked at her, touching her taking Melanie's hand against in her own. Their bracelets touched, and it was then when that Melanie felt herself begin to cry.

Holy fuck, she told herself as she cried.

"What's the matter?" Bailey asked.

"I'm just... I'm just in shock that I did it. This is the one thing I've dreamed of more than anything, to have that freedom, and now that I have it, it's quite different from what I expected. I honestly felt scared of reaching out, of trying to get past everything that was happening, and to finally live a new life. But, it's better this way. I'm happier this way," she admitted.

Melanie really did feel better. The fear of finally leaving her shitty family was conquered, allowing her to move on.

"You did do it. You know, I wish I had half the courage you did sometimes," Bailey admitted.

"How so?" she asked.

"Well, you seem too eager to hit the ground running, to make things right that like... I'm a little jealous at times. I just feel that if I had half the courage you did, I would've been so much better off. I'm just happy, that's all," Bailey replied.

"Yeah well, I wish I had half your spunk Bailey. You're just so perfect, and the fact that you came back into my life is the biggest present of them all," Melanie said.

"I did get both of us a present too. I was going to show you tomorrow but well, it's obvious that we need this now more than ever," Bailey said.

She gave Melanie an envelope, and when she looked at it, a curious look covered her face. She tore the contents open, realizing what it was.

"No fucking way," she said.

"Way. I got some tickets for us to travel to Europe together. I mean, you have your passport, right?"

"Yeah, I got that forever ago," Melanie replied.

"Good. Because I want to take you to explore the world, without having to worry about deadlines, people, or bitchy mothers. I wanted to give you a gift that would make you happy, and one that we could share together, because you're truly the best Christmas gift of them all," Bailey said.

Melanie felt like crying. She grabbed Baileys' hands, holding them there and shaking them.

"Babe, you didn't have to do this."

"But I did. I'm sick of people walking all over you Melanie. You finally stood up for yourself, and that's what made me proud. I know that you've always been timid, but I feel better knowing that you're happy. You've made me proud," Bailey said.

Melanie nodded, looking at her.

"Yeah, I'm glad that I did. I feel good," she replied.

"Good. I want you to feel great babe. I feel like, once you finally let go and realized your potential everything would be so much better," Bailey admitted.

"You helped me realize it Bailey. I love you. So much. I never knew I was capable of love until I met you. I just thought that I'd die alone, but I have you and I know for a fact that it's better this way," she said.

"Good. I'm so happy for you Melanie. I'm so happy that you finally managed to overcome your fears, to finally make your life as meaningful as it could be, and to finally just, be happy," Bailey replied.

Melanie felt tears of joy glisten against her face, the happiness she felt, making her feel happy and whole.

"Thank you so much Bailey. I love you," she said.

For Melanie, that was the first time she ever uttered those words, and to someone that she meant it for. She never forced herself to tell her parents that she loved them, because she didn't. They didn't care about her. Her mother was toxic, and her dad didn't do anything. But saying this to Bailey right now, made her feel much happier, more whole. She realized over time, that this was the beginning of a brighter future for both of them, and the beginning of something more.

"I love you too Mel. I'm so glad that I could make you happy. You certainly are the one for me, and no matter what, I'll be here for you. We've got this," Bailey replied.

Was this what it was like in those fairy tales where the two people would come together, confess their love, and then kiss and live happily ever after?

She didn't know for sure. It was so different compared to what she thought it would be, but in many ways, it was better. Happily ever after did exist, and she felt good about it.

Bailey leaned in, and Melanie pressed their lips together. Bailey was surprised by the sudden action, and Melanie enjoyed that. She kissed her passionately, the two of them exchanging their kisses with small, sensual touches. Both of them moaned against one another, and Melanie wondered if tonight, she could take care of Bailey. She pulled back, looking at Bailey with a smile.

"C-could I take care of you tonight? I want to make you happy, as a thanks for being there for me and helping," she said.

Bailey smiled at her and nodded.

"Go for it, but if you want to switch roles at any time, be my guest," she replied with a smile.

Melanie felt her heart lurch at those words, excitement obvious on her face. She pushed Bailey down on the couch, straddling her body as she kissed the brunette with a force that surprised even her. Desperation was obvious in her touches, the need for Bailey growing and growing.

She missed her, and that overwhelming feeling of happiness due to the fact that she didn't have to see her family again was something that made her feel liberated and happy. She continued to kiss her passionately, both of them letting their tongues mingle and touch with a desire that knew no bounds. Bailey moaned, and the sounds that she uttered while Melanie kissed her were delicious. Surprisingly, Bailey was cool with letting her take control, so Melanie took advantage of that, letting her lips mingle with Bailey's and the desire grow.

She pushed her tongue toward Bailey's lips, begging for entrance. Bailey opened her mouth, slightly surprised by the action, but pleasantly happy with the results as Melanie kissed her with a need that was bigger than she thought. She let her hand move up Bailey's legs, trailing up to where her thighs met, before she stroked the heat, feeling the radiant energy and the desire that grew.

"Fuck," Bailey said, lightly groaning in response.

"You like that, don't you?" Melanie asked, lightly teasing each and every single little crevice. The small touches were enough for Bailey, for even the subtle ones made her contort her face in pleasure.

Melanie loved this. She knew for a fact that Bailey did as well, but being able to take control, the desire to make Bailey feel as good as she did that first time, at the forefront of her mind. She then moved her lips toward Bailey's neck, lightly kissing.

"Be careful. I'd rather not wear makeup at the gym and at dinner tomorrow," she said.

Melanie smiled, lightly teasing the area.

"But it could be fun. We could have matching marks to remember each other," she purred.

Bailey groaned against her, and Melanie figured that was what the brunette wanted to do. Melanie quickly started to bite down, moving a small lock of hair so that she could get that perfect angle. With one little motion, she bit down on the flesh there, causing Bailey to utter a scream that she enjoyed.

"Holy fuck," Bailey cried out loud.

Melanie smiled, teasing the very edge of her skin, letting her teeth sink in and lightly bite down and nibble. She loved hearing the sounds, watching as Bailey flailed against her, the wanton sounds enough to drive her completely mad. She relished this, craving more of it, but of course, she didn't want her to cum just yet. That's why she kissed down her body, making her way to the blouse that she wore under the blazer. With little hands, she moved toward each of the buttons, carefully undoing every single one of them. She watched with delight as Bailey started to gasp, lightly moaning as she bucked her hips, and Melanie couldn't help but enjoy everything about this.

"Someone's turned on," she said, moving her hands toward the breasts that were in Bailey's bra. She teased them, kneading the orbs and exposing the nipples. They were bigger than her own, and Bailey was quite sensitive there. When she heard Bailey start to gasp, Melanie smiled, feeling superior as she continued to tease the tips of her nipples with delicate hands.

She touched them, playing with them, and as Melanie let her fingers move around the nipples, lightly pulling on them and teasing them, she watched with delight as Bailey started to gasp, bucking her hips up and forward as she continued this. For Melanie, this was arousing, and everything that she did to her turned her the fuck on.

Melanie wondered how much more of this she could take, but then, she quickly pulled off Bailey's bra, touching her flesh there and teasing. She moved her hands around the curvature of Bailey's breasts, taking a moment to eye the nipple before she took it in her mouth.

With small sucking noises, she went at it, watching with delight as Bailey began to moan. She continued to suck on the flesh there, letting her hand move toward the other nipple and playing with it. Everything about this was such a turn on, and for Melanie, she loved everything that she could give to Bailey.

The sheer notion of her getting turned on like this was mesmerizing for Melanie. She loved watching Bailey's eyes roll back slightly, a moan escaping her mouth, and the way her pussy seemed to lightly buck up in response. Melanie was transfixed by the way that Bailey's body looked. She was muscular, so her breasts felt more like muscle, and she was amazed by the way the sinews of the flesh seemed to make a perfect picture. Everything about this was just... perfect, and Melanie loved that she was the one who got to experience it all.

"Holy fuck, you have amazing abs," she said.

"Yeah, it's not much, but enough to be there," Bailey said with a blush. Melanie smiled, looking at the hard muscles. She began to move her tongue against the rippled edges of each muscle, teasing them. Bailey immediately cried out in surprise.

"Whoa!" she said.

"Anybody ever do this to you?" Melanie asked.

"N-no, that's why I was so confused, but I kinda like it. You can continue," Bailey said with a reddened face.

Melanie smiled, moving her lips amongst the trail of the flesh, listening with delight to the sounds Bailey made, and the way that her body seemed to fit perfectly in her hands. Melanie couldn't believe that this was happening, but then, she soon moved down to Bailey's thighs. She took off the stockings with care, watching as Bailey flushed against her. It was then when she started to kiss up her muscular thighs, eying how strong they felt in her hands. This was perfect for Melanie, for it was everything that she dreamed of. As she continued to move upwards, she looked at Bailey, who was practically begging for Melanie to continue, from the look in her eyes.

"Are you sure?" Melanie asked.

"Yes. I want this," Bailey said.

Melanie nodded, catering to her lover's wishes as she pulled her skirt all the way up, moving her panties to the side and the skirt to her hipbones. She could smell Bailey's feminine scent, and it was both arousing, and amazing to take in. She looked up at Bailey, who was already flush in the face.

"W-what are you going to do?" she asked.

"You'll see,' Melanie said with a smile.

She spread Bailey apart, her fingers exploring her flesh. It was different form her own, but it had the same touch, and as she let her hands graze against the flesh, she watched with delight as Bailey began to moan, trying her best to keep everything stifled. It was obvious that Bailey was so used to being on top that being on the bottom was a novel experience for her.

"You're enjoying it?" she purred.

"Y-yes," Bailey said, gritting her teeth at her.

Melanie smiled, letting an exploratory finger slip between her folds, all the way into her as she felt Bailey for herself. The touch was enough to make Bailey throw her head back and scream, and she watched with abject delight as Bailey started to move her body against the digit. Melanie loved everything about it, and she desired to have more of this woman.

She pressed her tongue toward the nub, lightly touching it, and as she stimulated Bailey's clit, she watched Bailey's eyes widen, her body shaking with delight, and it was amazing to behold. Bailey started to buck her hips, shaking with pleasure as Melanie continued to tease her. Melanie didn't expect Bailey to be like this, but then, she stopped.

"W-why," she said to Melanie.

"You have to beg for it, babe," she said with a smile.

Melanie watched as Baileys' eyes grew with those words. She could tell that Bailey had never begged for it either. She definitely was normally the one on top, but this time around, things changed, and it was obvious that Bailey liked it.

"P-please give it to me! I need my orgasm," she said with a small flush on her face.

The look that she gave Melanie was enough to make her panties wet with delight. There was something amazing about the way Bailey sat there, looking at her with such a wanton and needy face, practically begging for it all. It was delightful to behold, and Bailey seemed to enjoy this just as much as she did as well.

Melanie decided to listen, letting her fingers and mouth do the work once again. She let her lips move forward, touching that spot once again as she let her fingers move gracefully in and out, as if she was playing an instrument.

It didn't take long before she heard the delightful whimper that Bailey made when she was about to climax. However, instead of it being a simple little sound as before, she decided to fall back, let herself go, and when Melanie heard the moan that she uttered, she felt hotter than she did earlier.

It was the hottest thing, and Melanie couldn't help but feel aroused just hearing the sound. She pulled her fingers out, licking them and smiling.

"Did you enjoy that?" she asked.

"Yes, but I want to climax with you babe,' Bailey said.

Suddenly, the tables turned, and Melanie was pressed into the bed, their groins moving and touching against one another, a kiss of passion erupting from both of their mouths. Melanie enjoyed everything about this, completely enthralled by the way that Bailey suddenly took control. She pressed her fingers between her legs, pushing them in, letting her thumb rub her clit with soft strokes.

The sudden touch, the sudden action shared by the two of them immediately drew Melanie to madness. She shivered, clinging to Bailey and moaning out loud as she felt the fingers there. Melanie reached downwards, doing the same thing to Bailey, pushing fingers into her in the same manner. Bailey groaned, immediately pressing against her. Soon, both of their fingers moved at a pace quite different from what they expected, but one they enjoyed, nonetheless.

The two of them moved their fingers together, their tongues and bodies in a commingling that knew no bounds. Both of them craved the touch of each other and wanted nothing more than to experience the life they desired together. It was all Melanie wanted, to have Bailey in her life forever, and she knew for a fact she would definitely enjoy everything about this with the woman she loved.

The two continued to touch one another, their pace faster and faster, and it was then, after a few more strokes, Melanie tensed up, crying out loud and enjoying the sudden feeling. She tensed, her orgasm hitting her. When her digits gently moved against the spot Bailey knew and loved, Bailey shivered, crying out loud n pleasure as she came against Melanie's fingers.

Both of them climaxed together. It was something they both needed, that they both enjoyed. After a few moments, Melanie moved back, looking at Bailey with a smile on her face.

"Did you enjoy that?" she asked.

"Yes. I loved it so much Melanie. It was nice letting you take control," Bailey said with a smile.

"Well, I could do that again if that's something you like," she told Bailey with a purr.

It was obvious that Bailey liked letting Melanie take control, so Melanie would definitely do so again. She leaned in, giving Bailey a needy kiss, feeling enveloped in pleasure. They never wanted to leave each other, and it was obvious they would be together.

After a little bit, Melanie looked at Bailey, smiling.

"There was one thing I noticed here that was a little different from last time," Bailey said.

"What is it?" Melanie asked.

"You put up a Christmas tree," Melanie said with a smile, pointing in the direction of the living room.

She noticed the tree while they were making out, and she thought it was adorable that Bailey was doing all of this for her.

"Yeah, I felt like doing it for the first time this year. I'm happy to be here honestly, happy to have you Melanie," she admitted.

"I'm happy to have you as well Bailey," she said.

"You've changed me Mel. Honestly, I feel like everything is better this way. That I'm doing the right thing by confessing my feelings, and I want to have you with me forever. I know it's a ways off, but it feels nice, and I know I'll never leave your side. Honest," Bailey stated.

Melanie nodded. "i feel the same way. I won't either," she replied.

Melanie knew the beginning of their relationship would probably be rocky, but she was fine with the way things were going. She leaned in, capturing her Bailey's lips, and the two of them stayed like that. It was the perfect moment for her, and she knew this was the Christmas present she desired more than anything.

She didn't hear from her parents after her confession, but in truth, she felt better about it. She was scared to move on, but it was obvious that Bailey would be here for her. The touch that Bailey gave to her, the hand squeezing whenever she needed reassurance, it did make her feel happier. While she didn't have her blood family, the friendship they had before and the love shared now, was more than she expected, and she was happy.

Chapter Fifteen

Bailey hugged Melanie there, wanting to stay like this forever. She didn't want to let her go, but she felt the anxiety coursing through her body as she thought about tomorrow.

She'd see her dad for the first time in years, since he kicked her out of her home. It would be like what Melanie suffered, and Bailey knew that she needed to be there for the other woman, but she needed her own support too. It made it better for her, and she certainly liked it.

It also made bailey feel good about the future. It was a strange affirmation, something she liked having in the back of her head. Even with the slight worry, Bailey wasn't going to let it get the best of her, since she did have Melanie, and she felt more confident. Bailey didn't know what might happen.

She was definitely on good terms with her mom, but her dad was the one more upset about it than anyone. She wondered if there was any way to work this out.

After they cleaned themselves up, Bailey offered to put on a Christmas movie. Melanie agreed, and both sat down to watch the silly little holiday movie. Melanie seemed engrossed in it, but Bailey had her mind on other things. However, she could tell Melanie was realizing it but hesitated to ask what was wrong.

"You okay?" she finally asked Bailey after about twenty minutes.

"Eh, just a little anxious about tomorrow. I haven't seen my family in so long, I worry what they might say," she admitted.

"It'll be okay. Trust me on this. I think you'll do fine," Melanie said with a smile.

Bailey grinned back. She always had Melanie to count on to help her.

"Thank you. I do appreciate having you around. It makes life so much easier," Bailey admitted.

"Yeah, I feel that. I know that it's not easy, but you've got this," Melanie told her.

Bailey smiled, feeling excited about it all. She knew for a fact that Melanie was definitely here for her, so even if things did go south tomorrow, they'd work it out together.

"I'm just nervous. I haven't seen my family in so long, and it wasn't on the best of terms last time," Bailey said.

"You have nothing to fear Bailey. You're strong, and I believe in you. Trust me on this," Melanie said.

"I will. I'm so glad that you're here," she said to the blonde.

"Yeah. I am too. Honestly, even if things do go off the rails, I'm just glad that I got my Christmas gift, which was seeing you happy,' Melanie said.

Bailey blushed, leaning in to kiss Melanie passionately. The two stayed like that, letting their lips mingle and touch, then Bailey pulled back, smiling excitedly.

"Good. I'm sticking around too," she replied.

"Well, I am happy about that," Melanie teased.

The night was young, but both were happy. Bailey just wanted to feel this moment to last forever, to be with Melanie, no matter what might come next.

That night, after having sex once again, Bailey curled up against Melanie, feeling her soft body. This was something she could get used to forever, something that she wanted forever, but she didn't know if it was possible. However, she had a feeling that no matter the odds, no matter what transpired, things would be okay. They stayed in one another's arms, both of them enjoying the touch of the other, and Bailey had a feeling that, no matter what, things would be okay.

The next day, they got ready, and Bailey put in the address for her parent's home in her GPS. It was the same place, but it felt like a completely different time. She drove there, silent and worried. However, when she got there, she felt a hand against her own. She looked over, and there was Melanie.

"You have nothing to worry about," she said.

"Thank you. I do worry, but with you here, it makes life a little bit easier," Bailey admitted.

They walked to the door, and Bailey knocked. After a brief second, the door unlocked, and a familiar face appeared.

"Hey!" her mother said.

"Hey Mom. It's been a while," Bailey said, feeling the excitement in her body.

"Of course. I mean, I think you were like eighteen when you last were here. Time flies, doesn't it?" her mother said.

"Yeah. So, Mom, this is Melanie. My girlfriend that I told you about. Melanie, this is Lisa, my mother," Bailey said.

"I remember your mom," Melanie teased.

"And I remember you. You were always cheering on my daughter during basketball games. Who would've thought you two would reconnect years later?" she said.

"Yeah, I'm glad that we did. I don't regret a damn thing," Melanie said.

Hearing those words made Bailey smile. Her mother let them in, and soon, the two headed to the living room.

"Make yourselves at home. I did get you both a couple of gifts. Your father is in there too," Lisa said.

Bailey nodded, feeling the apprehension in her body. She had no clue what in the world would happen next, but after a moment, she stepped into the living room. Her father looked at the two of them, and immediately Bailey saw his eyes widen.

"You really did come back," he stated.

"Yeah Dad. Mom invited me over. It's been a while," she said.

"It has. Give me just a moment," he said.

He came over, hobbling a little bit, and Bailey realized that the fall had done a number on his body. But he still embraced her, and she hugged him back, happy to feel his presence.

"It really has been a while Dad," she said.

"Indeed. You've grown a lot," he said.

"Yeah. I'm sorry for what happened with the fall and everything," Bailey stated.

She figured just getting the elephant in the room out of the way would be fine.

He chuckled, slapping her on the back lightly.

"It happens. Nothing can take me down. We've been working on the company a lot. I know that we shouldn't talk business, but I heard you have your own personal training gig going on too, right?" he said.

"Yeah. I've been training Mom," Bailey replied.

"I should come in. This fall has left me so weak. I need the push," he said.

Bailey felt the tears well up in her eyes. Her dad didn't seem angry, and that was something that made her smile.

"Good. I would love that," she said, feeling her heart lurch.

"Anyways, have a seat. We can talk about the rest of that later when it's time," he stated.

They sat down on the couch next to her father, watching some Christmas movies and laughing, and Bailey felt a surge of happiness. This was the first time in a very long time she felt like she had a family, and there was something almost amazing about it. She didn't want this feeling to go away, nor did she want to ever take it back.

After a little bit, her mother came into the room, looking at the three of them with a smile.

"Dinner's ready."

They walked to the table, each of them taking a seat. Melanie moved toward Bailey, and Bailey felt Melanie take her hand, squeezing it slightly. It helped a lot, especially since Bailey felt the rush of anxiety that came with this.

After a brief minute, they started to eat, everyone enjoying it. Her father seemed happy, but it was obvious they wanted to discuss the past.

"So, Bailey, how is the personal training work?" he asked.

"Good. It's everything I dreamed of. I wanted this more than anything," Bailey said.

That was the reality of it. She wanted to have this type of life, and her father nodded.

"I see. So, you don't want to come to the company at all. Because I wouldn't mind leaving it in your care, even if it's just a temporary thing," her father said.

Bailey thought about it. She didn't know how to realistically take care of it. There were just too many parts to the company, and it scared her to even considering the notion of maintaining it.

"I don't really have the time to--"

"If you want, I can help take care of it for her," a voice said.

Bailey turned to Melanie, unsure what she was doing.

"But aren't you going to nursing school?" Bailey said.

"Yeah but, until I finish that, I need some work. Modeling isn't a thing anymore, so I'll need a job," she said.

"But--"

"Listen Bailey, I'll help you. And I'll make sure the company is strong. I did want to do marketing as well, and I guess if the winds take me that way, I'll do it. It's investing, right?" Melanie said.

Bailey and her father both looked at one another with shock on their face.

"But you just recently started dating my daughter," he said.

"Listen, I know that it's probably not conventional. I get it, I didn't expect this either. But for the first time, I feel free. And I want to learn new things. My family didn't allow that, so I'm taking advantage of the time that I have right now and doing what makes me happy. And if you want it, I can take your company and skyrocket it to new heights. You just need to show me how," Melanie said.

Bailey looked shocked. She couldn't understand why Melanie even thought about doing this. But, as if she read Bailey's mind, she spoke.

"Bailey, you do realize that you're living your dream right now, right? I want to help others. I've been living a lie, someone else's dream for so long, I don't know what to do about it. I've been going crazy, and honestly, if it weren't for you, I would've spiraled into the worst depression imaginable. I hate that I am so weak, but I know for a fact that with this, I'm happier. I want to help you Bailey, more than you could ever dream of, and I want to make it so that you're strong like me, and you're able to experience the dreams that you fulfill. Your business is so strong that it would be silly to leave it, but I have nothing. I literally just walked away from the most toxic experience I've ever had. Let me help you Bailey, and I'll help your dad too," Melanie said.

Bailey looked at her father, completely shocked by this.

"So, you'd really run the company with her?"

"Yes. I can do it. I just need to learn the ropes, and it'll be fine," Melanie told them.

Bailey was shocked at how sure she was. Melanie seemed ready for the challenge, ready for anything. Her father looked at Bailey, and soon, he spoke.

"Sweetie, you chose a fine girl to be with," he said with a smile.

Bailey was shocked by everything. She really didn't know what to make of any of this, but it did make her feel good. She smiled at her father, realizing that they did have the life that she wanted, and the one she enjoyed.

"Thanks Dad. I am happy too," she replied.

"Good. That's what matters. I didn't want to push it on you, but with my injury, I can't really work all that much. I wanted to give you the ropes, and if you didn't take them, I'd find another solution. But this works out well. I'll train Melanie here, to do everything that I need her to do. Thank you for that," he said.

Melanie grinned at him, and Bailey could tell that Melanie was happier than ever.

"I'm happy to help. Plus, I really do care about Bailey, so her issues are mine. I'm not leaving her behind," Melanie said.

"Good. I'm glad that you're able to help her like this. You seem perfectly strong, and you seem to be a fine woman for Bailey," he said.

"I'm surprised that you didn't get together sooner. I mean, I thought you were dating in high school. David did as well," Lisa said, looking at her husband who scratched his head.

"Yeah. I'm sorry for being so rude back then. I just...I didn't understand. I hope that you can forgive me," he said.

"I do Dad. Thanks," Bailey replied.

Her father smiled at them, and for the first time, Bailey felt like she was a part of the family. It was strange, transitioning from being abandoned by your own family, to being loved and cared for. But Bailey was more than happy about everything, and she was certainly ready for the future.

It was a nice feeling, that's for sure. She was shocked by the nature of it all, the way everything felt. It was like a dream come true for her, and when she looked at Melanie, it was obvious that she was just as happy as well.

They finished dinner, and then, David pointed toward the living room.

"We got you a couple things," he said.

"Thank you," Bailey replied. She looked at the bag in the corner, bringing it to her family.

"I got you both some something as well. It's weird bringing presents to people, since this is the first time I've done it on my own, but I'm glad that I've managed to reconnect with both of you. I don't regret a damn thing," Bailey said.

And she was serious about that. She didn't regret her choices in life. She felt like she was finally living the life that she desired. Her dad nodded, smiling at her.

"I'm glad that we reconnected as well. I'm really sorry for being an asshole back then, for forcing you to do all of that. I know that it wasn't what you wanted, but I learned my lesson. I can't let you stifle your dreams. You're happier than before, happier than when you lived here, and you've got a wonderful girlfriend, who I'm excited to have on the team," he said.

"Yeah, I'm glad too," Bailey replied.

She hugged her dad, and for the first time in a very long time, Bailey felt like she had a family again. She pulled Melanie over, and the group shared their first hug together in a long time. It made Bailey smile, made her happy, and she knew that no matter what happened next, she did have a family, one that would support her.

"You have our utmost support dear," her mother said.

"Indeed. Even if things go south in the future, just remember you have us, and you have each other," David replied.

Melanie and Bailey stared at one another, smiling excitedly.

"We do have each other. It's the beginning of a bright future, one that is perfect for both of us," Bailey replied.

They went to the tree, opening gifts together, and Bailey was in shock at how wonderful her parents were. They got her new equipment and clothes for her training business, and Bailey was happy to bring forth a gift for them as well. Melanie also got something, and Bailey thought it was the sweetest thing. They acknowledged her girlfriend, and she was so happy about that.

After everything, Bailey and Melanie went home. However, they hugged her parents, and Bailey felt love for the first time from both of them. She really didn't expect it to be like this, but with the way her dad seemed to care once again, and the happiness he seemed to exude, Bailey felt happy, and she didn't want this to ever end.

"Please don't be a stranger. Come see us whenever," he said.

Bailey nodded.

"I will definitely try to do it as much as I can. If not, you can always come to me for some personal training," she teased.

Her father laughed.

"I'll be taking you up on that very soon," he replied.

They parted ways, and when they got to the car, Bailey smiled at Melanie.

"That was the best visit I've had. I didn't think they would accept me back into their life with open arms like that. I'm just...shocked in all honesty. I thought they hated me," Bailey said.

"They don't hate you Bailey. It's very obvious they both love you," Melanie said.

"They do. But I have a few questions for you," Bailey said with a smile.

Melanie looked at her, and Bailey then took the plunge, asking the question she wanted to.

"Why did you decide to work with my father? I mean, I thought you wanted to go into nursing. Investments is definitely not nursing," Bailey said.

"Well, it's something I can do while going through clinicals, and if I end up hating nursing, I'm going to just go into that. It sounds like he knows what to do, and he's got a good head on his shoulders," Melanie said.

"Yeah, that's my dad for you. But...you want to do this right? You've been working a job you utterly hated for so long, that I want the honest answer as to whether or not you want to do this. I don't want to force you to do something you hate," Bailey replied.

Melanie shook her head, and Bailey's eyes widened.

"If I hated it so much, I wouldn't do it. I wanted to get out of modeling. It's a toxic place, and not something I enjoy. But, when I'm with you I... I feel happy," Melanie said.

Bailey felt a rush of happiness as she looked at Melanie with a smile.

"You're the best. You know that?"

"I feel better already. I'm not being forced to be on some bullshit restrictive diet, and I can spend time with you. I'm sure I could come work out at the gym you're at too, and I can become stronger," Melanie said.

"Yeah, I can help with that. And I think it's for the best that you do this. I mean, you're definitely happier, and you're going to be doing something you enjoy that's not too much work. And if you do decide to change it up, let me know, because I can always talk to my dad and we can figure it out," Bailey said.

"I think I'm happy with the lot I've been given," Melanie said.

"And I'm happy with you," Bailey said to her with a smile.

The two of them kissed passionately, and Bailey felt a rush of excitement knowing that she had this support network to rely on. Melanie mattered so much to her, and she felt a rush of happiness when she realized that she would indeed get to have Melanie like this. The two of them would work it out, no matter what, and when Bailey pulled back, a grin was the only thing that she could show.

"By the way, you're the best Christmas present a girl could ever have," she said.

"No, that's you. You're perfect Bailey, and I'm happy to be here," Melanie said.

Bailey felt loved for the first time, not just by her girlfriend, but by everyone. It was a novel feeling, but Bailey believed in love once again, and she knew that Melanie felt the same way. The two of them kissed one another with a passion that knew no bounds, and Bailey was ready for the future. They would create the best Christmas memories possible, and they would also make sure that the other was taken care of, no matter what the odds may be.

Chapter Sixteen

Melanie went straight to work after the new year, working with Bailey's dad. The investment job was certainly different from what she thought she'd end up doing, but she was quite happy with the results. She knew that it was something interesting, and honestly, even though she wasn't sure whether or not she should do it, there was a strange interest that didn't seem to go away when she worked with him.

Her father was strict, but he was also super nice. He let Melanie work the hours that fit her, so that she could spend time with Bailey. Plus, Melanie was also allowed to make as much money as she wanted, which was nice, because she was able to work whenever she wanted. Trading was pretty easy, and so was managing all of the investments.

After one of the shifts, he looked at her, smiling.

"You know, I don't think Bailey could do this any better. I'm glad that you decided to help," he said.

"I'm glad too. I mean, it's fun, and honestly, I kind of dropped nursing to get more education in the realm of business. It's weird not being decisive on your career, but it's nice at the same time. I get to try new things, and they're things I certainly love," Melanie said.

"Well good. I'm glad that you like them," he said.

Melanie went over to the gym after her shift, meeting up with Bailey who was finishing up with a client.

"There you are. Ready to lift?" Bailey said with a smile.

"Born ready. Plus, I get to work with the cutest instructor," Melanie said.

Melanie took up lifting after she finally got away from her mother. Her mom was always chiding her about doing this, mostly because she didn't want Melanie to look "Manly" but Bailey quickly told her that it wouldn't happen if she knew what she was doing. So, Bailey helped Melanie, and Melanie felt proud of getting strong. After their session, Melanie looked at Bailey and smiled.

"Thank you for everything," she stated.

"You're welcome babe. I love seeing you get so excited about fitness. It's a lot of fun, and I'm glad that you're here with me. I mean, I couldn't experience it with anyone better," Bailey said.

"Aww. Thank you," Melanie said.

She leaned in, capturing a kiss for a brief second before she slipped away. She looked at Bailey, smiling warmly.

"By the way, I think a date would be a nice little topper to this awesome day," Melanie said.

"I would love that. Want to hit a bar?" Bailey asked.

Melanie nodded. "Sure," she replied.

They were heading out, when suddenly, Melanie paused, seeing someone ahead.

"No way," she said.

Melanie realized it was her mother. She was in the cafe, looking directly at them.

"What the hell is she doing?" Melanie asked.

"Well, she's probably curious about what her daughter is doing. I mean, if she wants to say something, she can come to us," Bailey said.

Her tone was that of annoyance, and Melanie didn't blame her. This woman didn't accept her for who she was and was nothing more than a bitch. Melanie was tired of her, but she also wanted some closure. If she was going to play this game, then she would definitely want to make sure that things were said.

"Well, let's go talk to her," Melanie said.

"All right. Just be careful."

Melanie and Bailey walked toward the cafe, and Lara came out. She looked at them, and then, Melanie spoke.

"Mom, what are you doing here?" she asked.

"I came to apologize. I know what I did was wrong," she said.

"Yeah, you kicked me out. But I'm living a much better life. It's been almost two months since that day. I don't like you, Mom. I'm living a better life than you could ever imagine," she stated.

"I know. I figured you were happy. I was wrong though Melanie. I was wrong to force you to live my dream. It's obvious I fucked up, and I'm sorry for that," she said.

Melanie's eyes widened. Wait, she was sorry? Melanie didn't know how to respond to that, but then, Bailey spoke.

"Thank you for the apology. She is doing better, and isn't held down anymore," Bailey said.

"Yeah Mom, I'm happier. I don't want to go back to my old life. I feel...like everything is better now," Melanie said.

"Good. I know that I'm going to miss those gigs, but, it seems like you're better off. I...I wanted some closure," she said.

Bailey looked at Melanie, and Melanie nodded.

"Thanks Mom. Honestly, I don't want to go back to what we had in the past. In truth that's well, the past. It wasn't a good situation, in fact it was toxic, and it wasn't what I desired. But, if you do truly mean what you say, you'll let me continue to live," Melanie said.

"I will try. I just get worried, because modeling is all that you knew."

Melanie nodded. "Yeah Mom. I know that, and the reason I did only know that was because of you. It's not healthy for me, and since I've made this choice, I'm happier than ever. I'm not living your dreams anymore. I'm living my own life, my own happiness, and I'm not going to let my past get the best of me," she said.

Her mother looked at Melanie with shock. Melanie felt stronger though, happier than she'd been.

"I can't believe you found something better than modeling."

"Mom, I hated it, I didn't want to do it. I feel like...ever since I've made this change life has been easier. I did find something better than modeling. I'm still hesitant about letting you back in, but I'm glad you reached out," Melanie said.

"I do want to see you, and it seems like you're happier with her," her mother said with a slight bite of her tongue.

"Yeah Mom. I am. I made a decision for the first time ever, and if you want to be a part of my life, you have to accept bailey as well," she admitted.

The woman looked at Melanie, and then at Bailey.

"I see. I do want to try to learn about both of you, what makes this so special. If that's okay," she offered.

Melanie was a bit unsure about doing this, but when she looked at bailey, who seemed to forgive her even for what she did, it urged Melanie to do the same.

"Sure Mom. let's catch up in the future," she replied.

Her mother embraced Melanie, and for the first time, Melanie felt happy. It was such a strange, but such a nice feeling that she didn't want it to end. They started to talk, and it seemed like the hostility of the past was slowly dissipating.

Melanie wouldn't forgive right away, but the fact that her mother was trying, really trying, made her feel better about it all. The three of them went out to dinner, and although the atmosphere was terse, Melanie noticed her mother was laughing, having a good time, and really getting to know her. This newfound appreciation was different, but Melanie liked it.

"You two seem right for each other. I'm sorry for everything I said. I really am. I know I'm not the best parent Melanie, and I know that I hurt you, but if you could find it in your heart to forgive, I'd love that," her mother admitted.

Melanie knew it would take a little bit, but she was starting to understand. Bailey nodded at her, giving her a small smile.

"Yeah Mom. let's try again," Melanie replied.

"Good. I'll be a better parent this time around. I can promise you that," her mother replied with a smile.

The three of them finished dinner, biding Melanie's mom farewell. It was a strange feeling, watching the other woman leave, and the feeling of happiness that Melanie felt was so different, that she never wanted to let this go. She looked at Bailey, who was smiling, happy to have won.

"She's gone now. You don't have to worry about her. She's accepted her faults, and it seems that she's trying to understand you better. it's not perfect, but better than before. ," she said.

"Yeah. I'm just...shocked that's all," Melanie said.

"Your Mom did have some toxicity, and I can still tell, but she's trying. I say accept her actions as a means of understanding. Meanwhile my family accepts you. I accept you. It's obvious that you're not going to be happy if you keep doing this. You need to move on, and I'll help you," Bailey said.

Melanie nodded. "You already have and so much more. I know my mom isn't perfect, and she's trying. I believe her, but I'm glad I have support too. I'm happier just being around you, and I'm ready to face the unknown," she said.

"I am too. Remember, you're not alone anymore Melanie. You don't ever have to do anything that you hate, because you'll have me, and I'm ready to make your life the best that it can be," Bailey said.

The conviction in her voice was so obvious, and Melanie loved that Bailey was so sincere. It made her feel loved for the first time in forever, and it made her realize that the future was brighter than ever, and she could live the life that she wanted. She was able to do so with Bailey, who cared for her, wanted her by her side, and really cherished her.

"You're the best Bailey. I love you," she said.

"I love you too Mel. More than you'd ever know," she admitted.

Melanie felt a rush of happiness, pulling Bailey into her arms and kissing her at this moment. She didn't care if they were out in the middle of the street, or that people were watching. She was just...happy, and she was more than ready to continue to experience this happiness she desired, forever and ever.

For Melanie, having Bailey around was the beginning of a new future, and when she pulled back, she looked at Bailey with a grin.

"Ready to hit up that bar?"

"Hell yes. I need it," Bailey said.

They locked hands, heading toward the place where it all started, the bar where they met one another for the first time in years. It was obvious that their future was looking better than ever, and Melanie felt as if she didn't have to live in fear anymore. She wasn't forced to live a life she hated, nor was she forced to do things she didn't want to do. Instead, she had the comfort and security of being able to live her own life, to experience the freedom she desired.

And that mattered more to her than anything else. She knew that freedom was what she wanted, and the freedom she desired was provided by Bailey herself.

Made in the USA
Middletown, DE
06 March 2019